MW01038028

The Usual Desire to Kill

a novel

Camilla Barnes

SCRIBNER

New York Amsterdam/Antwerp London

Toronto Sydney/Melbourne New Delhi

Scribner
An Imprint of Simon & Schuster, LLC
1230 Avenue of the Americas
New York, NY 10020

First Scribner hardcover edition April 2025

SCRIBNER and design are trademarks of Simon & Schuster, LLC

Interior design by Kyle Kabel

Manufactured in the United States of America

10 9 8 7 6 5 4 3 2 1

Library of Congress Cataloging-in-Publication Data has been applied for.

ISBN 978-1-6680-6283-8
ISBN 978-1-6680-6284-5 (ebook)

The Usual Desire to Kill

Prologue

—I don't think much of those new socks of yours, *she says.*

—I never think of my socks, *he answers.*

—I looked at the label on them; it says hand wash only.

—And?

—Well, I'm not going to spend the rest of my life hand-washing your socks.

—It's unlikely that you will, although you may spend the rest of *my* life doing that.

June

One Saturday morning last summer I sat at the kitchen table, watching Dad out by the duck pond feeding the Bad Cats in the hot French sun. He walked back across the lawns, empty cat bowls in one hand, floppy garden hat swinging in the other. Despite his age he was long and loose-limbed. His hair still had an elegant wave to it and there was a distant glitter of the mischievous schoolboy that lingered in his eye. How like Alice, I thought. The same loping stride, angular and English but not awkward. He was followed by a couple of white ducks that waddled on their webs, burrowing their beaks in the lawn as they looked for worms. Once outside the kitchen, beneath the dusty vine, he stopped and took off his boots.

At the same time, on the other side of the house, Mum came in through the front door. She was wearing a dress—she would call it a frock—that I could remember her buying in England before they moved to France, so it must have been thirty years old. A splashy summer cotton of pinks and blues, it had worn well, but I could see that she had let out the darts in the back. She had always been sturdy and solidly built. Stocky, unlike Dad. It would have taken the same amount of Plasticine to make either of them but rolled out differently. Mum was like a piece of low-slung Victorian furniture: chubby cushions, thick brocade, dark wooden arms, and too heavy to move on your own. Nothing sagged—her face was plump, the skin taut and shiny, likc good-quality oak. Her clothes fitted as tightly as if a liquid form of her had been poured into them from above.

The kitchen was in a strategic position; I could keep an eye on both the back and the front of the house but at the same time stay tucked away in a corner of the L-shaped room. Mum was just back from the market—a heavy basket sat on one hip and a shopping bag weighed down the other. She couldn't see me as she hobbled in, put the basket and the bag on the floor by the small, squat, under-the-counter fridge, then groaned as she stood up straight. She called out to Dad. No one answered. She knew he wouldn't have his hearing aid in, but this didn't stop her. She blamed his deafness on a lack of effort. As she often said, "He just doesn't try."

She called again, louder and more crossly, "Hurry up! You've been out there for ages." Then waited for an answer, although she hadn't asked a question. "I got everything done. Everything that was on the list. On my own." Silence. "Where *are* you? What are you *doing*?"

Dad opened the back door and stuck his head in. He saw me but said nothing.

Mum looked up at him. "Don't put your boots there."

"I haven't put my boots anywhere. Not yet."

"Have you seen Miranda?"

"What?" He cupped his hand over his ear. And then he turned and winked at me.

"Miranda. Your daughter. Have you seen her?"

He thought for a while before answering. "I don't think so. Still in bed, I expect. Or no, actually, maybe I *did* see her. She went into town. Or was that yesterday?"

"*I* was the one who went into town, not Miranda."

"I'm sure she'll appear at some point." He came in and feigned discovery on seeing me. "Aha, there you are!" And then, to Mum, "You see? I told you she would turn up." I coughed and waved a silent paw.

Mum looked tidy but worn. She turned to face me as she busily sorted her shopping. As she did so, the buttons down the front of her dress strained and gaped, displaying eye-shaped holes of flesh. "I didn't see you skulking there. Did you have a nice lie-in?" This was her subtle way of pointing out that, unlike her, I hadn't got up at dawn. She didn't wait for me to answer but, with one sandaled foot, pushed the basket toward Dad. "You can put all that away." He knelt down and started somewhat randomly shoving the contents into the fridge. Mum surveyed proceedings, then suddenly dived in to pull a red cabbage out of his hands. "No, not *that*."

"You said *all that*."

"Yes, but obviously I didn't mean *all* that, did I?"

"Well, I'll just put all *that* in the fridge then, shall I? And not the rest."

"And this is for the freezer," she said, passing him a carrier bag.

"*All* this? Or just all *this*?" He took the bag from her hands and looked inside. "I sometimes wonder why we buy all this fresh food, if we're going to freeze it. I mean, maybe we should just go to the freezer shop to start with?"

"It's nice for the butcher; it keeps him going."

"Yes, but is it nice for *us*? Couldn't we eat some of it *before* freezing it?"

"You wouldn't know the difference anyway. I could give you cardboard and you wouldn't know the difference."

"That would depend if you cooked the cardboard first. Or would you freeze it? Now, if we had *fresh* cardboard, I—"

"Out."

Outside was what they liked to call the *buanderie*—in reality no more than a lean-to shed built against the kitchen wall. It was filled with old ice-cream pots, trays of seed potatoes, broken coffee machines. A shiny new freezer stood in one corner, draped with a length of faded brocade to protect it from the bats that nested above. She pushed Dad out and shut the kitchen door on him, still calling out instructions: "The *top* drawer, not the bottom where there's lots of room. I'm keeping that for my black currants!" Then paused, listening to him rummaging around outside, before starting up again. "And don't let the Bad Cats—"

Dad came back, the carrier bag—now empty—in one hand. "I put it all in the bottom drawer; there wasn't any room in the top," he said, as a feline stream rushed through his legs. The Bad Cats roamed the garden, never far from the kitchen door, continually planning a collective heist for a minute of warmth and biscuits. Hodge and Juno—the House Cats—were supposed to patrol the cat flap but usually just watched lazily from a distance.

"You've let them in! Don't just stand there. Hoosh hoosh! Out you go, all of you. The bottom? What did I *say*?"

Dad looked down kindly on the tabby swarm at his feet. "Yes, come on, out you go; do as you're told. We all do."

"Really, you let them do whatever they want. They would run the house if it was down to you. You'll have to go back and find space in the top. Go on; out you go."

Whether it was Dad she was talking to, or the cats, they all obeyed and left.

Mum had bought the original freezer in Oxford in 1971. A cavernous chest with a chocolate Formica lid, it was christened Boswell, after the shop it came from. As the years passed, the top faded to beige and no longer shut but was held down with a breeze-block. Its motor whirring and wheezing in constant effort, it had nonetheless traveled with them when they moved to France and had stayed there for over twenty years. In an act of generosity tempered with self-interest, after two decades of eating suspect food, my sister and I had finally bought a smart new vertical freezer as a birthday present for Mum. The deliverymen were under strict instructions to take Boswell away.

Mum was now squatting in front of the fridge. The door was open and she was busy excavating inside. "Your father, he's getting terribly clumsy," she said, over her shoulder. "And forgetful." I held out a hand to help her up, but instead she passed me a saucer of gray pâté that she intended to give us for lunch. No doubt Hodge had turned it down that morning. "And you really should say something to him about those dreadful slippers of his. They're not fit to be worn."

Dad came back in again. He was indeed wearing a pair of truly hideous slippers. Mum pointed at them. "You shouldn't go outside in those; you'll ruin them."

"You told me to go out."

"Yes, but not in those. You're old enough to manage your own footwear, aren't you?" Dad held up the carrier bag and raised his eyebrows questioningly at Mum. "Smooth it out and put it away, if you've finished going in and out like a cuckoo. Well then? Did you fit it all in? Those silly drawers, they're such a waste of space. Boswell was much more practical."

Dad handed me the plastic bag to deal with and wiped his hands dry on a tea towel. "Practical maybe, but at the end of what was a very long life. It would have been kinder to leave him to die in peace in England." Having bravely spoken his mind, he sat down at the kitchen table and pretended to be absorbed in a seed catalogue.

"Yes," I chipped in, "and you could have bought a new one over here, when you moved."

"We didn't *want* a new one; the old one was perfectly good. Built to last, not like things now," said Mum. "Anyway, we couldn't have left it behind. What would we have done with all the food?"

Dad raised his eyes from the glossy, tomato-covered pages. "Your mother is quite right; what would we have done with all the food?" It was often difficult to tell if he was trying to avoid marital conflict, or in fact stirring it up.

"Eaten it?" I suggested.

"We did eat it, but over here," said Mum.

This was true. When they left England, they had moved not only Boswell but also its contents. Still full of Sainsbury's chicken thighs, it had been unplugged, loaded onto a removal van, taken to Dover, floated across the Channel, then driven halfway across France, arriving ten days later. And plugged in again. This was, according to Mum, "perfectly safe" because it had been shut all the time it was in the truck.

She heaved herself up off the floor, inspected the pâté that I still held in one hand, then took a knife and began to trim away the crusty edges. "And anyway, that was twenty years ago and now I have your lovely new one. It was a very good opportunity to go through what was in it. I found some quite interesting things."

"Dead bodies," Dad suggested.

"Very old dead bodies," I said.

"Dodos."

"T. rex casserole." Dad almost laughed but put a hand over his mouth in time and went back to his seed catalogue.

"Very funny, you two. Here, if you're going to read that, make yourself useful." Mum thumped a pen down in front of Dad. "You can tick the beans we want. You do remember what kind we like, don't you?" She turned to me. "When my mother died, she still had a bucket of eggs in isinglass in the garage."

"Perhaps that's why she died," Dad said, flicking through the pages looking for beans.

"What's isinglass?" I asked Mum.

"It was a thing you did in the war. You had a bucket of isinglass, and you put eggs in it, to keep them."

"You see where she gets it from?" said Dad.

"I thought you didn't have eggs during the war."

"No, you didn't. So when you did, you kept them," she said, with implacable logic. "There weren't any real eggs. Only dried ones."

Dad hesitated, pen in one hand. Did they like longpods or Windsors? It was impossible to know. All he could be sure of was that he would be wrong. “Ahh! Dried eggs, yes,” he said to the world in general. “Tasted a bit like dandruff. But not as nice.”

“I’m amazed you didn’t all get food poisoning,” I said.

“Food poisoning?” scoffed Mum. “When I was little, people didn’t get food poisoning.”

“We didn’t have time to be poisoned by eggs in isinglass,” Dad said. “Diphtheria or polio got there first.”

Mum whisked away the catalogue with a, “If you’ve finished mucking that up,” and tucked it behind the fruit bowl. She had sent off the order form the week before.

“People say you are only supposed to freeze stuff for a few months, but think of Mallory.” We both looked at her, waiting for an explanation. “George Mallory. Everest, 1924. He still had his boots and all his bits when they found him in the ice eighty years later. If it’s frozen, it can’t go off.”

“I don’t think anyone was made to eat Mallory,” I said.

“Well, neither of us are dead.”

“Not yet, dear, not yet,” coughed Dad.

“I’ll have my coffee in the sitting room, thank you,” said Mum as she firmly put on her glasses, left the kitchen, and shut the door behind her.

At last Dad and I were together, unguarded. He got up and shuffled across to the coffee machine in his much-maligned slippers. “I wonder if she’ll put *me* in the freezer when I die?”

“No room for you in there, Dad.”

“In the bottom drawer perhaps, once we’ve eaten the bloody black currants. You know, I sometimes think that our stomachs must have evolved since we've had that awful machine. Adapted to digesting cheap meat, past its sell-by date, then frozen, thawed, and refrozen. Darwin. Survival of the fittest. I wonder if they had freezers on *The Beagle*?" He reached up and opened the cupboard above the sink. "Coffee? Mind your head, let me just—" A pile of cups and saucers slid out and crashed onto the floor. "Bugger."

He picked up a curve of thin, white porcelain and looked at it sadly, sitting on his palm. "I'm going to be in the Dog House now." He handed me the remains. "Put it in the bin. The outside bin, or she'll see it. Right down at the bottom. Underneath the bottles."

"I'm sure you'll get away with it. Unless she counts the cups before going to bed."

"She didn't notice the other ones."

"How *many* other ones?"

"It's difficult to say. Or actually, no, I suppose it's not that difficult. Look at the saucers in the cupboard. It's always the cups I break, never the saucers. And I never throw the saucers away, just buy more cups. And for every cup you buy, you get a saucer. So at some point she is bound to notice that we have seventy-eight saucers but only three cups . . . But perhaps I'll be in the bottom drawer by then."

After more than fifty years of marriage, they were set in their ways, like Mallory in the ice. It was a game of stubbornness versus pedantry and it was pointless trying to intervene. I watched as Dad struggled with the spaceship-like coffee machine. He eventually passed me two half-filled cups. I put the faintest hint of sugar in one of them and then took them both through to the sitting room, leaving him to make the last cup for himself.

Mum had put on an upbeat ragtime LP that Dad had always particularly loathed, despite not being able to hear it. He called all forms of jazz "ice cream van music."

Juno, the tortoiseshell, sat on Mum's lap, front claws firmly embedded in her thighs. "I can't get up." She waved at the coffee cup in my hand. "Put it on the mantelpiece. Careful of the clock."

"I've put sugar in for you," I said.

"I only like a little. Did your father turn off the coffee machine properly? The knob at the front *and* the switch at the back."

"I'm sure he will. Although I don't see why you turn it off anyway."

"What about that red light on the front? You couldn't leave that on; think of the electricity you'd use."

"I think if you left it on nonstop all year it might use a euro's worth by Christmas."

"Exactly my point."

Dad came in and picked his way carefully over the various slippery rugs. "Where's Hodge?" He looked at the empty stool by his armchair. Standing by the cold grate, he held out a cup to Mum. "Here."

"I've already got mine!" she said. "That one's yours. And be careful of the clock."

He put the cup on the mantelpiece, moving the softly ticking carriage clock to one side. It had been an engagement present, all those years ago. He looked puzzled. "No, this one can't be mine. I put sugar in it."

"It's only sugar. And only a little."

"I'll go and make myself another." He picked up the cup again.

"You're not going to throw it away, are you?"

"Of course not. That would be wasteful. I'll drink it while I make a new one." He turned to leave and, one hand on the door, said to me, "Very nice dinner yesterday, wasn't it, Miranda? Your mother calls it *blonket de vo*. I think of it as stew, personally. What did you think of the *meat*?" He gently shut the door behind him. Mum looked at me, waiting for my answer.

"Very . . . tender?" I said.

A triumphant smile spread across her face as she ran a firm hand down the back of Juno's knobbly spine. "Veal cutlets, out of the freezer. 1983."

July

Perhaps before I go any further I should give you a cast list. We are not a very reproductive family, so it will be short.

Dad: Retired professor of philosophy in his late seventies.
Mum: Wife of the above, two years younger.
Charlotte: Early fifties, daughter N°1.
Miranda (*that's me*): Not quite fifty, daughter N°2.
Alice (*my daughter*): Not quite twenty, a chemistry student.

I was twenty and still at drama school in London when I decided to move to Paris. I wanted to be an actress and felt the need to escape England and all of the above (except Alice, who didn't as yet exist). In many ways, acting was already an escape from reality, but that wasn't enough for me; I wanted the distance to be measurable in miles. I was barely out of the country when, rather unexpectedly, Dad took early retirement. He had always complained about foolish, flippant undergraduates who wouldn't know the difference between philosophical logic and the philosophy of logic—even if they were sitting on it. Now, he said, he had had enough. He would waste no more time on others but would devote his latter years to himself and thinking about what he mysteriously called "valid inference." My parents sold the tall redbrick house in North Oxford where they had been living since I was born and followed me to the continent.

They bought a large, dilapidated manoir that stood in an overgrown garden on the edge of a hamlet in rural France. Civilization (the railway and shops) was half an hour from there, in Poitiers. At the time, neither of them could drive and it was clear that one of them would have to learn.

The house was called La Forgerie and was made of local, creamy white stone with a slate roof and a tower at one end. It was built in the early 1800s and since then, other than the installation of various bathrooms and lavatories, nothing much seemed to have changed. Although imposing when viewed from the garden, with its three floors and rows of tall windows and pale gray shutters, the house was not quite as vast as it seemed. On the other side, where the gravel drive drew up, there were no rooms but only long, windowed corridors. This gave the house a bit of an old railway carriage feeling. On the ground floor were set out one after the other: the kitchen, staircase, dining room, sitting room, and music room (containing nothing but a single untuned and untunable upright piano), each room with its own marble fireplace, oak parquet, and high ceilings. On the second floor, a similar series of four bedrooms and two bathrooms. And at the top, under the eaves, the former servants' rooms, all linked together with doors leading from one to the other and now entirely given over to Dad's library. There was a sagging sofa and a creaking wheelie chair in front of the desk with his computer. Maps of ancient Greece hung on the walls between the bookcases. The floorboards were unwaxed and there was no nonsense about heating arrangements; that wouldn't be good for the books.

At the far end of the house was the drafty tower. It contained nothing but a second staircase that was cluttered with broken dining chairs and piles of newspapers tied up with string. Wildlife was abundant; bats, wasps, mice, and once a red squirrel had all nested there. Tendrils of creeper covered the rarely opened shutters and wormed their way inside.

In the first few years of residence they put up wallpaper on the ground floor, installed a new boiler, mended the roof on the duck house, and had a tennis court built on the top field. They also adopted two llamas called Lorenzo (usually referred to as Lollo) and Leonora who would come and watch when we played tennis. Games usually pitted two parents against one daughter. It was always Mum who kept score—in her own idiosyncratic fashion. The llamas' long necks turned left and right, watching as we humans inexplicably hit what looked like apples at each other.

This activity of home improvements first waned, then stopped altogether. As time passed, fewer friends from England came to stay. Some were too old to travel—it was an inconvenient place to get to—others had died or moved abroad. Bedrooms and bathrooms were shut down one by one and I could imagine a point in the near future when the two of them would be living in a bedsit in the middle of a vast manor.

By this time I had become a competent but uninspired French actress. I must have been twenty-five or twenty-six when I found myself onstage in a professional production for the first time. The play was *The Seagull*, but I was Masha and had little to say. I imagined Mum and Dad coming to see the show. In my mind's eye, they sat unsmiling in the stalls in their buttoned-up coats and hats, sore thumbs in a sea of happy faces. I was worried; from the stage, how could I *not* look at them? How could I not be distracted by their parental gaze? Afterward, would they say what they really thought? Would they offer encouragement, even if they had slept steadfastly through three hours of Chekhov? Would there possibly even be a glimpse of parental pride at seeing me onstage and being applauded?

I needn't have panicked—they never came. There was always a good reason not to: on one occasion they were saved by a rail strike; on another Dad had a nasty cold. And then when it was at last convenient for them to come, they discovered that the run was over and it was, "Oh! Too late; we missed you!"

I, on the other hand, came to visit them quite often. A weekend, rarely longer. I lived in Paris and it was only a couple of hours on the TGV. It's not that I felt that I should, or that I wanted to, but I felt that I ought to want to, so I did. But, as Dad would say in his philosophical way, what did I mean by *ought*?

Over the years they had evolved a well-rehearsed technique for living together. It was a two-hander play, but there was also a bit part for me. Like two pieces of a broken plate that didn't in fact fit together and never had, they used me not as glue but more as a translator; I often found myself communicating the desires or complaints of one to the other.

My sister, Charlotte, was four years older than me and we had always been startlingly different in most ways. When we were little, she had a long straight, impossibly perfect plait that hung down her back. I used to dream about chopping it off when she wasn't looking. My own unruly hair was always cut as short as short could be, by Mum in the kitchen, with the kitchen scissors. We grew up and Charlotte had the plait cut off herself, but our differences remained. She lived on her own, safe in Bicester. (Yes, she was my sister in Bicester, a tempting first line for a limerick.) Her children, two sporty boys, were grown up and their father had been removed from the equation years ago. The geographical distance that now existed between us helped to transform our sibling rivalry of the past into a strange sibling unity. Our parents—the very thing that had once kept us apart—now brought us together. As they aged, they became our overlap, our common ground.

Charlotte rarely felt she should come to France. Or perhaps she felt that she should come rarely. Either way, the result was the same.

Writing to Charlotte had become my way of venting the frustration accumulated after a weekend in La Forgerie. Catharsis, I suppose, would be the correct term. Mum would have called it making a fuss about nothing.

From: MIRANDA
To: CHARLOTTE
Date: Tuesday 17 July 2018 at 11:15
Subject: Off to Bolivia

Just a quick letter as I pack my rucksack. I have finished the current production I was in. It was a terribly dull play, but that's an actor's life; you take what you are offered and then you complain about it. Tomorrow I have a flight for La Paz via Lima, arriving the next day. I have taken plenty of warm socks and four volumes of The Jewel in the Crown to read; that should keep me going in the Andes. Oh! A whole month of tramping across the Altiplano, going there on my own, not having to worry about other people or other actors, it sounds like bliss to me.

It was another long and depressing weekend in La Forgerie. Mum was on good form as ever. The morning conversation was about the new freezer (Boswell was much better, etc. etc.; you know the story . . .) and how wasteful the two of us are. ("It wasn't like that during the war; we never had sweets, or bananas or chocolate. It was jam yesterday, jam tomorrow, but never jam today.") Does she think we can't count? Anyone would think that she was the one who lived through the Blitz, and not Dad. She was only a baby when the war ended, although I suppose she would remember rationing. Have you heard of "eggs in isinglass"? No, neither had I. I looked it up; it is something gelatinous involving fish bladders. Revolting.

After lunch on Saturday, she came up with a cracker. I was washing the knives—by hand as usual since it "spoils the handles if you put them in the dishwasher." It's not good for the forks or spoons either. And the plates are delicate; we must be careful with them. And we don't put glasses in, because the machine scratches them. So saucepans and cat bowls go in the machine; everything else you do by hand, with the same filthy sponge that used to be yellow when it was bought in 1965 in Shergold's. Anyway, there I was washing up, and I rubbed my eye with a soapy finger because it was itching. In a moment of madness, I told Mum that I thought I had a sty coming on. She bustled over to me and prodded my eye with the finger she had doubtlessly just used to open a packet of slug pellets. "Oh yes, it does look a bit red. I've got some ointment I can give you for that." There was no point in refusing. Off she went to look in "the medicine cabinet" (= rusty old biscuit tin) in the cupboard under the stairs. She came back with a small, wizened metal tube with a long pointy nozzle—you know, the kind where the paint has gone all scaly and fallen off, so you can't read what it says. "I'll just go and do it in the bathroom mirror," I said. I went upstairs, slammed the bathroom door, waited a couple of minutes, and then came back down, said thank you, and asked where to put the tube. She pointed to the box on the kitchen table. I picked it up; on one side was shakily written in Biro (and this is true): "Twice a day, for Cornelius." So I was being offered secondhand ointment that had been prescribed for a cat that died five years ago. I showed it to Dad, who said, "Put it away and say you used it, thank you very much. It's easier that way. Much easier."

I put the tube in its box, the box in the biscuit tin, and the biscuit tin back in the Ali Baba cupboard under the stairs where I found, on top of an impressive collection of light bulbs, rusting aerosols of oven cleaner, old rags, and silver polish:

- a lifetime supply of plastic bags rammed into another, larger plastic bag
- a box of old syringes once prescribed for a boil on Dad's leg
- 17 rolls of baking paper (all partially used)
- an impressive collection of string, different lengths and thicknesses and colors, wound up in individual little skeins

- a selection of devices for killing flies, wasps, moles, and mice
- an abandoned toaster with two slices of toast still in it
- an iron with an English plug
- a hair dryer with no plug

No newspapers, empty jam jars, ice-cream pots, or egg boxes, you say? No, of course not; these are stored outside in the *buanderie*, where there is more room.

A brief exchange from breakfast you may enjoy:

Dad: Why do the cats get the posh, fresh milk and we get the UHT stuff out of a box?

Mum: They don't like the other kind.

Dad: Neither do I.

Mum: You don't like *either* kind. You never drink milk.

Dad: That's not the point.

Or what about this, between me and Mum sitting on the sofa after lunch:

Mum (*reading the newspaper*): It says here that there's a new Steve McQueen film coming out. That can't be right; he's dead.

Me: Maybe you are thinking of the wrong Steve McQueen.

Mum: Steve McQueen. *The Magnificent Seven*. You know—da da, dum di da *da*, da da, dum di *da da*. Maybe you're too young. But I'm sure he's dead.

Me: That's Steve McQueen the *actor*, not the director. It's a different person. This one makes films; he doesn't act in them. He made a film about slavery in America. It was called *Twelve Years a Slave*. He's black. And he's not dead.

Mum: Don't be ridiculous, Steve McQueen isn't black. At least, he wasn't in *The Magnificent Seven*.

It has to be said, they may be barking mad, but I always come home with some good anecdotes.

Back in Paris now, safe and warm and *not* dead from food poisoning,

Love,

Miranda

PS. Still not dead, but check up on me tomorrow . . .

◆

Oxford, October 1962

Dear Kitty,

Dear, dear Kitty! Oh how lucky I am. A new world beckons. New friends and no family. How lucky I am to be here and to have you. It would be hopeless trying to write to John and Matthew, quite hopeless, and you know it would. They are both perfectly charming, but they are silly young things and of course they are brothers. Whereas you are a sister. And ancient and wise. I say that in the kindest possible way—I know you're not that ancient, but you are older and wiser than me. And you have already left home, so you understand.

To start with, I was expecting a clean, sweet city lulled by ancient streams, but what I got at the railway station was a Wimpy and overflowing dustbins. Coming in on the train you could be anywhere, it was so drab and depressing. The station wasn't at all like home with the stationmaster and his cat and his pots of bulbs you mustn't sit on. No one talks to you here; they all rush around because they know where they are going—but I don't! I asked someone the way and they pointed vaguely over a bridge and to the left, so I followed the finger and trudged along in the rain, with cars swooshing past me and soaking my legs. Actually, no, they didn't swoosh past me; it was one big traffic jam all the way. The cars and buses just sit and shudder gently. By the time I was standing in front of the address they had given me I was wet from the outside and the inside; my vest was itching, my stockings were runkled up at my ankles, and my hair was in the maddest of frizzes. There was a stone archway and a wrought-iron gate, shiny black and gold, with the college crest high above my head. I walked across the flagstones but couldn't see a bell, so I pushed the door (more shiny black paint) and it swung open. Once inside, things were less glamorous. I went into the porters' lodge and gave my name to a grim old harridan. She checked in a ledger and then rather grudgingly showed me upstairs. "Bathroom here, lavatory here. Cold water only, not to be wasted, not to be used at night. Careful of the carpet here; there's a missing stair rod." Then I was left to myself.

I sat down on the hard bed (They call that a mattress? More like sleeping on old toast) and suddenly it came over me. Here I was, in my own room, with my own window and my very own little key in my damp hand. I took off my hat and looked out of the window. Something Gothicky was sticking up over the tops of the trees. I wildly decided to fling open the window and immerse myself in Oxford. Well, I didn't quite fling it open—the sash cord was broken and I had to give it a great bash with the back of my hand, like doing the gate to the pony field—but at last it gave way and a gush of gray air came in: a mix of lime tree and petrol, damp boots and cold tea. I was here.

xxx, Your Loving Sister.

Oxford, early November 1962

Dear Kitty,

I know I'm not stupid, but I also know that I'm not <u>that</u> clever—I mean not clever enough to have been accepted if Kind Unk hadn't stuck his finger in and stirred things up. He didn't say as much to me, but I'm sure he must have got my name moved up the list, what with all the people he knows here. You should see what the other girls look like. So serious, so sensible, so determined. I suppose you have to be like that if you're a girl—we have to prove we deserve to be here, whereas the boys (or men I should say; they have bristles and pipes) just take it for granted. We don't see much of them and of course we're not allowed out after ten, but our paths do cross, now and then. They seem to spend more time on the river than in the library—if you can row you don't need to be clever. An option not open to ladies—rowing is deemed "inappropriate." Or, at least, it's all very well <u>rowing</u>, but certainly not <u>racing</u>. Whereas if you're a man you have to race and not row.

I must accept that, if I am to get along, I must be more serious and sensible than the men. I may row, but I may not race. I must work as hard but expect less; I must accept that I will have less than more. All the ones I have met so far are like Mr. Toad; brash and noisy. Mostly they are straight out of top-notch schools and think they have a right to all this—and all that it will give them later in life. Before coming here I never thought about where I stood on the ladder of life. I thought I went to the right sort of school, but I'm not so sure now. I'm not sure about anything anymore. The Mr. Toads of life, they are sure. They just march on without looking over their shoulder—they know they have the right kind of clothes, the right kind of hair. They mess about in boats and read the right kind of books. They will be all right, no questions asked. What about me? Poor Mole coming out of his house after spring cleaning! Will Ratty come along and show me the river? I don't know, not yet.

What do you think? Will I manage?

xxx, YLS

Oxford, late November 1962

Dear Kitty,

I am the only one here who has homemade clothes, but no one talks about that sort of thing. They look, but they don't comment. There is no one to tell me if I have laddered my stocking or have a hole in my glove. In fact, no one wears gloves; it's not like school at all. I noticed yesterday how particularly awful my skirt was. When I started making it, HQ said I should cut it out with an extra inch all around the pattern pieces, so there would be "room to grow into." Does she think that at eighteen I am going to grow into anything? Perhaps sideways but not upward. There must be an age at which you can no longer grow into something, whatever it is. You are what you are and that's it. The result is very lumpy at the waistband, and I was never really pleased with the way the zip went in so I always pull my woolly down over it. Still, it's the best skirt I have and the only one made out of material that was actually bought for the purpose, rather than being cut out of an old overcoat or the curtains from the nursery. I think of it as my going-away skirt—and I can put the hem up, now that I have indeed gone away.

Best of all here is that no one talks about the war. Back at home it was all anyone could talk about—the war the war the war the war. Well, I can't remember the war, and I don't care, we were miles away, on a different continent, and it was ages ago anyway. I wasn't born and we weren't in England, and even when we got back it's not as if we were living in Coventry or London—surely Hereford was just the same after the war as it was before?

You're so lucky; you knew the first house, before Hereford. Before England. I wish I had. I have seen the photos; the wedding, with Pa and HQ standing in front of the school in dappled light, both in their best suits and not smiling. And there is even one of me, a tiny prawn-like baby, perched on HQ's bosom. You agree that she has a bosom? No other word will do. I cannot think of her as "Mother" or "Mama," but expecting us all, including Pa, to call her HQ is a bit odd really, isn't it? Headquarters, where everything is decided and organized. She leaves no space for warmth, for comfort, for belonging.

"The strange-scented shade of the great dark carob tree"—is that right? I do wonder what a carob tree looks like. Did I belong there? I suppose that is the point of having an Empire—it being different from home, I mean.

Here everyone is either too young, like me, to talk about air raids and bombs, or so old and crusty and busy with the crossword that they can't remember what they did yesterday, let alone twenty years ago—and they would have been too old to fight then anyway. No, that's not really fair; they aren't all that old—in fact, my tutor is quite young and breezy—it's just that everything seems as if it has been here for centuries—and it has—and that the war was just a blip and is already forgotten.

There's a photo hanging in the corridor by the porters' lodge of when they used the college as a hospital. On the frame it says: "1943: Hospital for Head Injuries." There are two nurses standing up in white uniforms with red crosses on their chests. In front of them, sitting down, are two servicemen. One is in uniform and boots, the other in his dressing gown with a blanket on his knees, so he must be the Head Injury. You can see drips and iron beds on wheels behind them, and what's funny is that this is all out in the garden at the back—you can even see my bedroom window with the broken sash cord. Do you think they wheeled them out every day for fresh air, or did they make them sleep in the garden? I sometimes wonder if a Head Injury died in my room. If they did, I hope they did it romantically and not messily.

All that anyone can talk about here is the new bypass that might or might not be built (so not romantic or intellectual at all). Everyone agrees that it is a Very Bad Idea. But then everyone said the same thing about the railways in 1830. And probably the same thing about any other invention since 1066 except the printing press. The essence is that nothing must change. I had an argument about the bypass with an old don. I said, "But if there was a bypass it would be easier for people to come here, wouldn't it?" And he answered, "But you see, we would rather that other people didn't come." Which sums up Oxford pretty well. (I have just thought that I could have said, "But isn't that the point of a bypass, so that people can pass you by?" I always think of these witty replies a day too late . . .)

xxx, YLS

Oxford, December 1962

Dear Kitty,

Such a funny thing happened last week, I have to tell you about it. I was on Cornmarket, looking in my bag for a missing glove (yes, I know I said no one wears them here, but I just can't quite lose the habit, not yet) when a car juddered to a stop next to me. A middle-aged man in an overcoat leaped out from the passenger side, all in a muddle, with a clipboard in one hand, his briefcase in the other, and his hat in the third one if he'd had one. And then a gawky young man in shirtsleeves and a fancy Fair Isle tank top staggered out of the driver's side—he looked terrible, all green and white and frilly at the edges like a Savoy cabbage. He stuck out his hand to say goodbye to the man with the clipboard and just then a huge stream of vomit came shooting out of his mouth and splattered all over the clipboard man. As I watched, little bits of carrot slipped and dribbled down his coat and onto his shoes.

I offered him my hankie and tried to mop him up a bit, but a hosepipe was what was really needed. Cabbage Man came over, looked at the two of us, then rushed off without a word, leaving poor Clipboard wiping the brim of his hat. I shook out my hankie and said I thought I couldn't do much better.

Clipboard said, "I didn't think he would take it that badly."

"Take what badly?" I said.

"It was his driving test today and he was doing quite well. I was just about to pass him when a dog dashed across the road in front of us. He didn't swerve or panic; he didn't even brake; he just drove into the poor beast."

That was when I looked at the car, and it was true, there was a sort of doggy smear all down one side and a spatter on the wing mirror.

xxx, YLS

PS. When I said it was a funny story, I didn't mean about the dog dying, I meant about the vomit.

November

Scene I

The curtain rises. It is lunchtime.

At either end of a long, waxed cherrywood table sit a couple. They are on high-backed dining chairs and no longer in their prime. An array of wine coasters, pepper grinders, and silver candlesticks separate them. Two cats sit on the table; each watches the action from its own cork-backed table mat. The tortoiseshell licks cream out of a spoon held by her mistress. The tabby, next to his master, closes his eyes and purrs sphinxlike.

—The vet is coming tomorrow. In the afternoon, *she says.*

—I thought Miranda was, *he answers.*

—Yes, Miranda for dinner tonight; the vet is tomorrow.

—Oh. More wine? (*He passes the carafe.*) What for, the vet?

—To do Lollo's toenails. But I want him to look at Leonora too. It's the right time of year and she's got that look in her eye.

—You should have warned me he was coming. I've got my ear appointment tomorrow. I won't be here.

—But *I* will be here and I will tell you what he said. (*She puts the cream spoon down.*) That's enough, Juno.

—We can move Leonora and the baby up into the top field, when it's born, for the summer. Lollo can stay down here so that he doesn't get in the way. What shall we call it?

—Get in the way? He's like you, no interest whatsoever in his offspring. When Miranda was born, you only came to see me in the hospital three days later. I had to think of a name for her all on my own. I could have sold her to the circus by the time you turned up.

—You wouldn't have got much for her. She was an odd-looking thing. Not much better now.

—You went off into college on your bicycle, leaving me on my own having a baby. I was all on my own with Charlotte.

—How can you be on your own, *with* someone?

—Try living with yourself; then you'll find out.

—I didn't know it was a baby. I thought it was the chop suey from the night before, coming back to haunt you.

—I had forgotten that. We had been to see *The Tempest*. And afterward we had dinner at the Blue Lotus.

—Wasn't it the Dear Friends? And *Titus Andronicus*.

—Definitely the Blue Lotus. And it could only have been *The Tempest*. Miranda. What would I have called her if it had been *Titus*?

—*You* were Titus, after that bottle of rosé, or whatever we had. Titus a Newt. That was what I thought was coming out the next morning.

—It was a baby, not a hangover.

He stands up. The tabby cat opens his eyes, stretches, and hops down from the table. He opens the door to the kitchen and Hodge slips out through his legs.

EXIT

◆

The summer had passed.

There had been a two-week heat wave in August and the llamas had suffered out in the sun. My parents had decided to move the two of them into the shady kitchen where they spent their days spread out on the cool tiles. They each had a bucket of water next to them and Dad brought them their breakfast and tea. Usually it was just vegetable peelings and some grain, but on lucky days it would be pineapple. A llama, even when it tucks its feet away tidily, is a large beast, but when I asked Dad how they had managed he said, "Oh, there was plenty of room for us; we had breakfast standing up. Leonora did eat a tea towel, but Lollo was perfectly well-behaved."

In October Mum had been to England for a week to see old friends and to stay with Charlotte. Left on his own, Dad had begun a new gardening project: digging up all the brambles in the hedge around the llama field. He dug them up one by one, armed with a single daisy fork and plenty of rage. Leonora and Lorenzo would wander over and stand guard, nibbling the hedgerows as he silently dug. They were not pets, a word that Dad disapproved of since it would imply that they belonged to him and were in some way beneath him. He felt responsible for all the animals that lived in La Forgerie, but the responsibility was that of a butler and not of a master. He didn't interfere in their lives, in the same way he didn't interfere in his daughters' lives. He was just not very good at being interested in other living creatures, particularly if they only had two legs. The more legs the better, he would say. He would be happier living with a spider than with Mum, if the spider could cook. A millipede would be paradise.

Evenings in La Forgerie followed a scenario dictated by Dad. He found living with other people complicated, incomprehensible; to help deal with their nonsensical structure, he held on to strict social values from the past. Once he had set out the dinner rules, he always obeyed them, even if he was on his own and after a bramble outing. You had to dress for dinner—you could wear whatever you wanted, but you had to change from what you were wearing before. There were drinks—always called drinks, or drinkies by Mum, never aperitifs—champagne if Dad could think of anything to celebrate and he usually could. There was obligatory conversation along with drinks, for which he was willing to wear his hearing aid and sometimes even turn it on.

Before dinner, he had to "Do the Ducks." This meant taking a pot of chopped-up stale bread out to the garden and shaking it while calling in a low quack. After a minute or so, there would be an answering quack, then the bobbing heads of eight white ducks would appear from out of the undergrowth and they would waddle toward their elegant house. A miniature version of La Forgerie, it was built in the same cream stone and came complete with a window, shutters, and electric lights. The slate roof was finished off by a stylish but rusty weather vane. Dad would turn the light on, wave the ducks inside, and then go in himself to fill their water bowl and tip in the chunks of bread. The ducks would wait a minute or so as the bread softened and became spongy. Once they had sat down to eat, he went out and shut the door but left the light on. This was what he called their Reading Time. He would go back later, before pudding, to turn their light out and say good night. As he did so he always said—to the ducks, to anyone willing to listen, or to the night sky above—“Put out the light and then put out the light.”

Dinner was first course, main course, then—after putting the ducks’ light out—cheese and pudding, or just pudding. There was a complete change of crockery and cutlery at each stage. Dad dealt with the meat or fish and Mum served the vegetables. There was a joint of meat if Mum thought Dad deserved it. Stew of some kind if he was in standard bad favor. If he was in the Dog House it would be fish, and if it was squid you knew that things were really bad. At one end sat Mum and Juno, at the other Dad and Hodge. The visitors (i.e., me) sat at the net and passed hot plates like boiling tennis balls from one side to the other. The cats were silent spectators but no doubt kept score. In winter the candles were lit. A large amount of wine was consumed whatever the season. By the time we sat down for the first course small talk was muddled by the “drinkies.” By pudding time Mum would be quoting French poetry and Dad staring at the ceiling, an earpiece dangling out of one ear, a pained but unwavering smile on his face.

Today was a meat day but not carvable meat, so just one step above the Dog House. Dad fished around in the stewpot, scooping out mangled bits of skin, bone, meat, and the occasional length of string, then passed the plates to me to pass to Mum who served the vegetables.

She added an extra piece of unwanted broccoli to my plate and opened hostilities. "Now, let me tell you about Oxford. Oh, and Bicester! Did you know that your sister now belongs to a Book Club?" I said nothing; Mum would answer her question for me. "Neither did I! At least she didn't offer to take me there. I was too busy anyway."

She had been looking forward to seeing her old friends but had found the journey depressing and tiring. She had expected to find them as she had left them, years ago. Instead, they were all looking older, balder, fatter, than before. "But then they have to live in Oxford, don't they? So they would." I pointed out that there were worse places to live—not to mention that she herself had lived there quite happily for many years. "All those glum neo-Gothic houses with huge drafty rooms, no bathrooms, and dreadful gardens full of araucarias. I always hated that house we lived in."

"We didn't have an araucaria. Surely it was a beech tree?"

"No, it was an araucaria."

"*And* a beech tree? Maybe there were both . . ."

Mum was not one to negotiate. Better to change the subject. "In those days there just weren't many houses for sale; you got what you could. It wasn't the same."

Dad, silent up till now, pounced on this last remark. "It wouldn't be the *same*. It couldn't be. Only similar."

Mum pretended not to have heard. If you got into an argument with Dad, you could only lose. You might innocently say something along the lines of "It's time to go" and he would say, "What do you mean by *time*? Did you mean 'It is *time*' or 'It *is* time'? If you meant to say, '*It* is time,' then I would question what you mean *It* to be." And so on. The "same or similar" argument was a frequent visitor.

"As I said," Mum went on, brushing Dad out of her hair with the back of her hand, "it wasn't the same."

"Different," I said. "Not necessarily *worse*. Just different."

By that time Mum had U-turned back to trees. "There was definitely an araucaria in the front garden in my grandfather's house. Not that I ever went there." She closed her eyes and considered the question for a while, one hand wrapped around her wineglass. I could see her mind ticking backward, back past the war she never knew and then further back to the previous one. She opened her eyes again. "A glittering future he had; it was tragic."

When Mum spoke of the war, it was with a hint of frustration; she had missed the exciting bits of her life. She was born in what was then a British colony called Southern Rhodesia, but the family was repatriated at the end of the war when she was still only a baby. She had no memory of Africa and had never been back. When she was little, people talked endlessly about the daring feats of the war: the daily struggle for survival, the refugees, the mass destruction, and the final victory. Even Dad had one up on her here—born in London in 1941, he could just about claim to remember the bombs. She had been bequeathed the dullest bits—rebuilding, rationing, the grayness of the fifties. England had been left a smaller, poorer, grimmer place, an Empire on the decline. In her disappointing family there were no tales of heroics, no uncles parachuted into occupied France, no brothers killed in action. For that she had to go back to the previous war.

"Gallipoli. Someone told me that it's called Gelibolu now. But that's ridiculous; it's Gallipoli. It's like saying that Salisbury is Harare, or whatever they want to call it. But it wasn't and it isn't."

"I think it wasn't, but it is now," Dad suggested. "You were born in Salisbury, the capital of what *was* Rhodesia, but if you went back now you would be going to Harare, the capital of what *is* Zimbabwe."

"I can't see why they want to change these things; what difference does it make?" Mum continued.

"To them or to us?" Dad said. "What about East Germany?"

"What does it say on your passport, Mum? Salisbury, or Harare?"

"The DDR," said Dad. "I have been there, but I couldn't go back, could I?"

"Well, Mum?" I said. "Rhodesia or Zimbabwe?"

"Stop it, you two; you are confusing me. I was telling you about your grandfather—no, I mean *my* grandfather, your *great*-grandfather. Whatever you think the place is called now, when he was there it was Gallipoli and of course they all got terribly shot up on the beach. They called it an amphibious landing, which always made me think of newts when I was little. He was so young. As I said, it was tragic. I don't think my mother ever got over it. She adored him."

I thought about this for a while. I already knew the story. It is 1915. Great-Grandfather is sent to the Dardanelles with the Hampshires, survives the absurd campaign without a scratch while the rest of the men are slaughtered; they admit defeat and withdraw; he is shipped home, gets peritonitis on the boat, and dies on arrival in England. But I had never given it close inspection, let alone questioned it. How could our grandmother have been "terribly fond" of her father, if he had died when he had only just got back from Gallipoli? She couldn't have been more than a baby.

"But how old was she, then?" I asked.

"Sixteen or seventeen. It was in the thirties."

"In the *thirties*?" I made a quick calculation in my head. "But you said he came back from Gallipoli and died on the operating table."

"Yes, that's right."

"Oh, I see, you mean 'he came back from Gallipoli and'—comma—'twenty years later'—comma—'died on the operating table'?" There was a long silence. Mum said nothing. "Dad?" I said. "What do you think?"

He had heard that last bit of the conversation. "I don't think you necessarily need the commas."

After defeat at Gallipoli, Mum went back to the safety of trees. "Despite the araucarias, it used to be quite pretty. Oxford, I mean. There weren't all those bankers from London. The undergraduates were a much better class. You should see them now! Pop music in the May Balls. In my time we had proper music, and proper dancing. You were *held* by your partner; it was quite something. Not that your father ever danced—he just smoked his pipe and read his book. And now they have to have coffee the whole time—not just coffee, but all sorts of complicated kinds of coffee in huge cups that they lap at. In the street. Sitting on the pavement. When I was up, you couldn't go into town without your hat and gloves. I had a lovely blazer, plum colored, with gold braid. And matching knickers . . ." Her voice trailed off and she put down her wineglass, suddenly not so sure of herself. "Or perhaps that was at school? I didn't have a blazer at Oxford, did I?" She took another generous sip from her glass, then moved back onto more stable ground. "You certainly couldn't have coffee in town. You could get a cup of tea—the tearooms, on the High, what were they called? It'll come back to me. There was The Mitre, if you wanted a drink, but I didn't, not then." (Dad, in the distance: "She's caught up since then.") "And there was a café in the cinema, which was called the Ritz then, not the Odeon. There was Shergold's, for hardware—I bought a blue enamel potty there, for Charlotte. I still have it; I start off my tomato plants in it; they do very nicely. If you wanted olive oil, you went to the chemist—they sold it in tiny bottles; it was very expensive. In the covered market there was a place that sold foreign food—avocados, anchovies, that sort of thing. There wasn't anywhere you could have coffee. But we didn't want it then."

"Or maybe you didn't know that you *could* want it?" I said.

"You sound like your father." She topped up her glass. "Aren't you going to eat your broccoli?" My plate was a mess of entrails and undercooked vegetables. "It's from the garden! It's my broccoli; you must eat it."

Dad wouldn't let that pass. "You said it was Miranda's. You said, 'Aren't you going to eat your broccoli?' It can't be hers *and* yours."

Mum rolled her eyes in frustration. "It's on *her* plate. Or maybe you think that's your plate, not hers?"

"It certainly is my plate. But I am lending it to her, on a temporary basis, for dinner. And if it's *your* broccoli, I don't think that she should eat it. In fact, Miranda—" His eyes glittered, and I could see he was going to stir things up. "In fact, I forbid you to eat your mother's broccoli."

"What about if I give it to her?" said Mum. "I'll donate it. It was mine, but now it's hers. Whoever's plate it's on."

Mum looked questioningly at Dad, who carefully considered the proposition and then passed judgment.

"It's in our house and on our dinner table; that makes both the plate and the broccoli ours. But if she does eat it, once she swallows, it will be hers. Unless she's sick in the night. Perhaps the vomit would be ours again. But only when it is out of her mouth and actually hits the bucket."

"Please, Miranda, leave the meat if you don't want it, but eat the broccoli and then he'll shut up."

I had been hoping that Mum would say something about her hip, but however bad the acoustics were in the dining room she wouldn't mention it in front of Dad. She had had a hip replacement five or six years ago. The operation had been done in France and they had warned her that the other side would need doing in the near future. It was clear when I watched her move that we were now there—in the near future—but Mum was very prickly about the question. She had only mentioned it to Charlotte, who was the official Doctor in the House, never to me (I was the Artistic One, Charlotte the Scientific One). I knew that Charlotte had arranged an appointment for her to see a doctor while she was in England, but I couldn't ask about that now with Dad hanging around. And anyway, Mum didn't know that I knew about the appointment, and Charlotte had ordered me not to let on that I knew.

I crunched up my last piece of semi-raw broccoli and asked Mum if she had seen Alice while she had been in Oxford. It was still French university holidays in October and I knew that she had been over at the same time as Mum.

"Oh yes, it was funny seeing her in England; usually I only see her in Paris. She does look French, doesn't she?"

"That's not really surprising, is it? She *is* French. Or at least her father is. Was."

There was an awkward silence. They didn't like Alice's father to be discussed. Charlotte's ex-husband was equally no-go territory. It wasn't necessarily the husbands who were shameful, but their daughters' incapacity to hang on to them. They were one of our many failings and it was a subject to be kept firmly shut up in the family freezer.

"I took Alice to buy a birthday present," said Mum. "I gave her a very good-quality coat, not that she said thank you."

"But you enjoyed yourself?"

"It was tiring, but yes, I suppose I had a good time. And I saw a bit of Charlotte—for once, she was there. Usually when I turn up she announces that she's going to another continent."

"That is her job, going to different continents."

"Air hostess, a job? Pouring tea, you mean."

"You're supposed to say 'flight attendant' now. And anyway, she isn't a flight attendant. You know very well she isn't."

"She has a uniform, and a badge with her name on it."

"That was thirty-five years ago, Mum. It was a summer job, when she was twenty. She's still at British Airways, but in human resources. You know she is. She's a coordinator or administrator . . . or advisor. One of those words."

"She used to hand out those horrid little wet wipes that smell of industrial lemon."

"She probably earns twice as much as Dad did. And anyway, you keep those lemon wipes when they hand them out to you on the flight."

"Of course I do. You never know when they might be useful. Well, as I was saying. We went to the theater; Charlotte had bought tickets. She does have odd taste; it was a terrible play. A waste to be in the stalls, for that."

Dad coughed his way back into the conversation. "Is it better to be in good seats for a bad play, or in bad seats for a good play?"

"And I bought some Marmite to take home," Mum went on. I couldn't stop myself telling her that you can buy Marmite in Paris. They have it in the supermarket opposite me. "Yes, maybe, but it's not the same thing, is it? I mean, the labels may look the same, but they put different things in, for foreigners. Now, is there enough of that meat left for another dinner or do you want some more?"

Dad put the ducks to bed; then there was cheese with apple tart, all washed down with wine. Then clearing up, coffee, and more wine. Mum finally staggered upstairs, one hand on the banister, the other on her hip. Dad shooed the cats out, took the coffee cups through to the kitchen, and shooed the cats out again.

The two of us went up, turning out the lights one by one as we went. I watched as Dad shuffled along the corridor into the flickering gloom of their bedroom at the other end of the house. In the bathroom, I swept the dead moths off the basin, brushed my teeth, and undressed. As I was getting into bed, I discovered that there was no bulb in the bedside light. I got partially dressed again, went downstairs, and rummaged around in the cupboard under the stairs. I beat my way through the dusters and the mousetraps, clearing a path to the light bulb section. I found something that seemed suitable, came back up, put the bulb in, discovered that that one didn't work either, gave up, and got into bed with the main light on. I rang Alice. She gave me her account of choosing her birthday present.

"Grandma decided that we didn't want to go all the way into town, it was too much bother. So we only went as far as the shops on the Cowley Road. She wanted to buy me something to wear, so we went into Cancer Relief, and then Sue Ryder. In Sue Ryder there was this bomber jacket that I picked off the rail and showed to Grandma, but she had already found a coat that she liked. She said it would be more useful. It's not really my style, but you might like it. And it would probably fit you. It's way too big for me, but Grandma said I would grow into it. And when we took it to the till, she said that she would pay for *half* as a present. But that she didn't have her bank card on her, could I pay for it now, and then she would write me a check when we got home. Which she did. But I've lost it."

"So basically," I said, "your birthday present was a second-hand coat from a charity shop that was too big for you, that wasn't the one you wanted, and that you ended up paying for?"

"Yup. That's it."

"It sounds like Rosamond and 'The Purple Jar.' "

"The Purple Jar" was a story that Mum used to read to us. It came from a terrifying collection of cautionary tales called *The Most Unfortunate Day of My Life*. It went, as I remembered it, something like this: It is Rosamond's birthday and her uncle is coming to take her to a flower show in the afternoon. This is clearly a special treat. In the morning, she goes into town with her mother to choose a present.

Now what Rosamond really needs is a new pair of shoes, but before going to the shoe shop they stop at the chemist. While her mother orders something at the counter Rosamond sees, high on a shelf, a beautiful jar. A deep purple glass jar. Could she possibly have the jar as her birthday present, instead of shoes? That, says her mother, would indeed be possible. Rosamond may choose. But she should take into consideration that she *needs* a pair of shoes, whereas the jar, pretty as it might be, she could *do without*. Rosamond dithers, but finally the purple jar proves irresistible. The shop assistant takes it down, wraps it up in rustling white tissue paper, and slips it into a box that she ties up with string. Rosamond proudly carries it home where her uncle is waiting. When he sees Rosamond in her shabby old shoes, he refuses to take her to the flower show and after lunch they drive off without her. Left on her own, she does at least have the purple jar to enjoy. She carefully unwraps it, planning to set it on the shelf above her bed. She notices now that there is something inside. She takes out the stopper; it is full of a dark, syrupy liquid. She empties the jar into the sink but realizes that, once empty, the jar is no longer purple, but just plain, ugly glass.

I was rather terrified by the story at the time and only began to question it much later. Why would the shoes be a birthday present? Surely if she *needed* new shoes, they should be bought for her as well as the purple jar. And what an awful shit the uncle was! Perhaps he was in league with the mother, who sounded hard as nails. She hadn't warned her daughter of the consequences if she chose the jar ("It's the jar *or* the flower show, Rosamond!"). And did no one think to tell her when she saw the jar in the chemist that it was full of purple goo and not actually purple itself?

The moral of the story was: Don't choose what you desire; choose what you need (or maybe what you think you ought to have, but what do you mean by *ought*?). Choose what your elders and betters tell you to. They are older and therefore they are better.

"You should have put your foot down and chosen the bomber jacket," I told Alice.

"I just paid up and shut up; it seemed easier."

From: MIRANDA
To: CHARLOTTE
Date: Friday 16 November 2018 at 23:18
Subject: Saint Bartholomew

Back in La Forgerie! It's always more depressing as winter approaches. In the summer you can at least sit out in the garden, which I can't do in Paris, so there is one positive element to the trip. Now, in November, the three of us are confined to the sitting room, flicking through the growing piles of *Country Life* and the *TLS*. There are more and more tobacco holes burnt into Dad's armchair and less and less color to the sun-bleached cross-stitch antimacassar. We sat by the fire, but it wasn't worth lighting it "because it's not that cold, is it?" Well, yes, it *is* that cold, I inwardly scream. Upstairs in my bedroom this morning delicate petals of frost fanned the inside of the window.

The general direction of things is slowly downhill—physically, but not mentally. The animals are in better shape than the humans, but then of course they have more time and money spent on them. I now beat them at tennis far too easily—and so easily that it's impossible to let Dad win a few service games for his own self-esteem without him noticing. Mum's hip is clearly bad and she barely moves on the court, but she doesn't let on. She likes to suffer in silence—it's a bit like playing tennis with Saint Bartholomew. He was flayed alive, but being a martyr, he never made a fuss about it. He wouldn't make a very good tennis partner. Mum would tell him off for dropping bits of skin on the court ("Such a messy saint, very inconsiderate. I won't have him to stay again!") or if he left his flaying knives lying around. Would he be allowed to put them in the dishwasher, or would it spoil the handles?

Now, your October mission was clear—do something about the Hip. I know that you had set up an appointment for that, but she said nothing about it to me. Please tell me how it went. She says it "isn't that bad," which is meaningless (more Saint Bartholomew)—if it's bad, do something about it; if it's not bad, shut up and stop complaining. Not that she complains; she doesn't. It's more like spectator martyrdom—moving in a certain way to make sure that I notice and feel sorry for her and then, if I ask, denying that there is anything wrong and doing sod all about it.

She made a rude comment about your driving skills (yes, I know—kettle, pot, etc., etc.) and gleefully told me that you had broken your wing mirror while she was there. Didn't she also break her wing mirror recently, I asked, when she was parking? "Oh no," she said, "that was quite different. I had a nasty cold and my ears were all bunged up." I couldn't quite follow her logic, so asked for a full explanation. "I was backing into a very small space in front of the chemist, but because of my cold I couldn't hear properly, so of course I couldn't see where the other car was parked. It was only the wing mirror. I don't know why they make them stick out like that; it's asking for trouble." Had she got it mended? I asked. "No, I thought it wasn't really worth it. Most of the time the car is in the garage, so I don't actually use the mirror that often."

Dinner tonight ended this way:

Dad: Is there pudding, or cheese? Or *and* cheese?
Mum: After all that beef?
Dad: Oh, it was beef, was it? I thought it was stew.
Mum: It was rather a rich sauce, I thought.
Dad: So just pudding?
Mum: You don't want cheese then?

She sent Dad out to the kitchen to get some water biscuits and asked me about my walking trip to Bolivia. I was about to say, "Bloody cold," but she had already changed the subject back to how awful it had been when she was staying with you.

Dad came back holding up a packet of Carr's all covered with spiderwebs.

Dad: These ones? They look a bit old. What's it say . . . Ha! March 2003!
(15–0)
Mum: You haven't got your glasses on. Let me see. Look, that's an eight. It says 2008!
(15–15)
Mum: Anyway, they're water biscuits; what can go wrong with them?
(15–30)
Dad: They look a bit soggy . . .
(30–30)
Mum: Better for your teeth.
(30–40)
Mum: If you had thought to warn me that you wanted water biscuits, I would have put them in the oven to dry them out.
(Game Mum)

You know that story about our great-grandfather in Gallipoli? Well, it turns out that the truth is not at all what we thought. Yes, he *was* in Gallipoli, and yes, he *did* die of peritonitis when he got back to England. But . . . twenty years elapsed between the two events. It's not quite the same thing, is it? You will say that it makes a better story the other way—but certainly not a more accurate family tree. Speaking of which, how are you getting on with ours? I bet you will find other chunks of family history have had the same treatment as the Gallipoli story. Aunt Bea will come up with some bits from the past for you. And what about The Incident? You must dig into that. You are the one who is interested in other people, not me. There's no point asking Mum. And no, I won't ask Dad.

After Gallipoli and cheese, we had a very good conversation about llamas, which of course she knows far more about than I do—but then this is true of most subjects. I asked whether she knew where Bolivia was (remember she used to think that Jaffa was in Spain because that's where the oranges come from?), but she was prepared for that question.

"I found it in the atlas; it looks horrid."

Yes, that's the huge *Times Atlas* that sits on the piano but is never opened. It's full of British Empire—the sun never sets on nearly every page. Surely clinging on to this ancient edition is symbolic of their life? An age of deference and dominance when everything was pink and people knew their place. Mum has never left Europe unless you count Zimbabwe ("No, it's Rhodesia!"), but even so she knows more about South America than I do. For example, she knows all about the llamas that live on the Altiplano:

Me: They have lots of llamas in Bolivia.
Mum: No, llamas live in Peru.
Me: That's not very far from Bolivia.
Mum: Oh no, Peru is near the sea.
Me: Well, anyway, they have llamas there. More llamas than you. And alpacas, vicuñas. And the other kind, whatever they're called.

Mum: Guanacos.

(So you see she's right; she does know more about camelids than I do.)

Me: Whatever. Up on the Altiplano. Great gangs of them, standing there in the middle of all the rocks and snow with nothing to eat and no mittens. It's bloody cold. They are much woollier up there than yours.

Mum: Ours are *very* woolly.

Me (*not giving up yet*): But in Bolivia they are woollier.

Mum: I was brushing Lollo last week, and *pounds* of wool came off him.

Me (*slightly losing patience at this point*): Yes, expect you're right. They weren't *that* woolly. In fact, some were almost naked. The famous Bolivian Nude Llama, it's a breed apart. I took some photos of them, prancing across the Andes, all goose pimples and singing "El Cóndor Pasa" in chorus.

Mum (*dryly*): Don't you want to show us some of your photos? You usually turn up with hundreds. Your father and I were looking forward to that.

She is the same as ever, but worse, whereas Dad has changed. When you think what he used to be like! We didn't see things the same way then. Your parents are your parents: you don't question what you have for dinner, or where you live, or how they talk to you; that is just the way things are. It's when you're older that you start to think, "Hey, that was a bit odd, wasn't it?" Alice has never seen him being cross; she can't even imagine it. She laughed when I tried to explain. All those thunderous but silent rages and not talking to us for weeks. Would it have been less awful if he had hit us? No, I agree, that would have been worse, but the fear would have been easier to recognize and deal with. At some point, he stopped being cross—or he was still cross, but it didn't show as much; he hid it better. Maybe it was living in a house with three women that made him angry. You would say that it is linked to The Incident. And you're probably right, in some way. The Incident—another mystery! We both have our own theories.

Love,
Miranda

From: CHARLOTTE
To: MIRANDA
Date: Saturday 17 November 2018 at 07:18
Subject: Re: Saint Bartholomew

Yes, sorry, I have been meaning to write a full account of the October visit for you, but I have been whizzing around the world recently. Hiring and firing, as they say. As you can imagine, although she only stayed a few days it felt like a lifetime. On the first evening I had friends for dinner—I think you've already met Patrick and his dashing husband? I had of course warned them about her before they turned up. When they arrived, she was already a bit tipsy and gushing, and as soon as they walked in she rolled her eyes and said to Patrick, "Oh, but I love Julian and Sandy in *Round the Horne*! Are you *that* kind of poof?" He didn't really know what to say to that and she went on, "I always say there are three kinds of pooves—bitchy queens, butch ones with moustaches, and pinko wrist droopers. So, what kind are you?" At least she didn't say, "I think it's so sad you can't say *gay* anymore. It used to be such a *nice* word."

She has really declined since the last time I saw her. Yes, she is seventy-something (seventy-five in April?), but even so. She walked at a snail's pace, tottering along in shoes that are too small for her, and out of breath after only a few steps. She can't really go up and down the stairs and getting out of the sofa takes ages. She calls it "taking my time." She did confess that her hip is much worse. So I said how lucky it was that I got her that appointment, the surgeon is a friend of mine, he's agreed to see her while she was in England, etc., etc. She claimed I hadn't told her about it before (totally false; I still have the email I sent her) and she refused to go. "Oh, it's too much bother" and "I'm not going all the way to Abingdon to see a doctor." Full stop. I thought I would kill her there and then. I told her that the longer she leaves it the worse it will be. She said, "It's not worth doing at my age." It's the same with her glasses—she clearly needs her eyes tested, but when I asked she said, "Why would I want new glasses? I've had these for forty-seven years and they have always been very good." Maybe if she had new glasses she would discover a new outlook on life (and maybe that's what she's frightened of).

Despite all that, I extracted a promise from her to go and see a doctor in France and to at least get an X-ray done and see if they can operate. She must be able to go back to the same place as last time? She doesn't want me to say anything to Dad about it, and nothing to you either because she thinks that you will tell Dad (which you probably will). So please remember, if she says anything to you about it, that I didn't tell you anything . . . It's the usual web of lies, you see.

She's worried that Dad couldn't cope on his own if she has the operation because it would mean not driving for several weeks. Yes, the world will be a safer place. They would be stuck out in the middle of nowhere without a car, but if they get organized and do a big shop before, they should be fine. They could eat what's in the freezer. Or in the larder. You could live for a year just on the horseradish sauce, unless it poisoned you first.

Love, C.

PS. Do you think I should talk to Dad about it?

From: MIRANDA
To: CHARLOTTE
Date: Saturday 17 November 2018 at 08:07
Subject: Re: Re: Saint Bartholomew

Re your PS—No, it's none of our business.

From: CHARLOTTE
To: MIRANDA
Date: Saturday 17 November 2018 at 08:11
Subject: Re: Re: Re: Saint Bartholomew

Re your Re PS—It will *become* our business.

On Saturday afternoon, I took Dad to have his hearing aid seen to. Mum stayed at home waiting for the vet who was coming to see the llamas. We were back in time for tea, which we had in the kitchen while the rain poured down outside. Dad didn't like tea, but Mum didn't like him drinking coffee all day because it wasn't good for him. So on Saturday afternoons he would make a large pot of Earl Grey for the two of us and a small pot of oolong for himself. He would pour himself a cup of almost transparently weak tea and let it cool down, while Mum and I thirstily scalded our mouths. Once we had finished our Earl Grey, he would collect the cups and pour his oolong down the sink. This technique seemed to satisfy everyone concerned.

Mum asked how we had got on in the Ear Shop and Dad said, "It was the usual girl, and as usual I couldn't hear her questions. So I answered randomly. Randomly, but wittily."

"Just like here then. Except you can hear me, you just don't listen."

"What was that, dear?" Dad stirred his oolong and Mum sipped her Earl Grey. "What about Leonora? What did the vet say?"

"Oh, I almost forgot to ask, we spent so much time tussling with Lollo's toenails. But he thinks probably not. That she isn't, I mean. Anyway, we don't really want more llamas, do we?"

"Well, I do," said Dad.

"What would you do with them? I mean, a baby a year is what she usually produces and I only just managed to give away Lucinda last year. What would we do with another one?"

"Keep it. We could keep it."

"Where would we put it?"

"There's plenty of room."

They had about seven and a half acres of land. At the moment there were two llamas, eight ducks, five chickens, and two official House Cats and it was difficult not to agree with Dad; there was room for an extra llama or two. Mum didn't see it that way: "Two is more than enough."

"But I don't want 'enough.' " He waved his teaspoon in protest. "Ideally I would have sixty-four. If I had sixty-four llamas I would be in what Epictetus calls ataraxia, a state of stoic calm. Aristotle thought that ataraxia was unattainable but that you should strive for it anyway. That the point of life was that—the striving for perfection. I know that I can never dig up all the brambles in the garden, but I can bloody well try. He says that even if I know that I can never have sixty-four llamas, I should strive for them and this will make me happy. Whereas Epictetus says that I shouldn't even *try* to have sixty-four llamas, since I never will. I should shut up and be happy with what I have."

"Clearly Aristotle didn't have to look after his own llamas, did he?" Mum sighed. "Epic-thingy had more sense."

"He had no sense at all. He was a fool and he didn't even make any good jokes. He said, 'We have two ears and only one mouth, so we can spend more time listening than talking,' which is clearly rubbish in my case. Actually, that would be a good name for a hearing-aid shop, Chez Épictète. Although I might be the only person to get the joke. Forget Epictetus. Aristotle is right. He is always right. I must aim for sixty-four llamas. I have calculated that with two llamas having one baby a year it will take a minimum of seven years to get to sixty-four. That's only if all the babies are female, and if all of them are pregnant once a year and as soon as they are born, which is unlikely of course, but not impossible. Like flipping a coin and getting heads sixty-four times in a row. Quite possible. But it would be bloody hard work for Lollo. Now, if only half are female, I wonder how long it would take to get to sixty-four . . ."

Dad was spinning off into one of his possible universes, where llamas roam freely and he stands in a state of stoic calm in a bramble-free Elysian field. Mum never believed in stoic calm, but in common sense.

"As I said, two is more than enough." And she poured his pot of oolong down the sink.

◆

Scene II

Early Saturday evening. It is dark.

He comes back in from the garden, stands in the doorway, silent, still in his boots.

He is holding an empty llama bowl in one hand.

—Have you done the hens yet? *she says.*

He doesn't answer.

—. . . There's some boiled potato they can have.

He still doesn't answer.

—. . . And you can take a couple of lettuce from under the cloche; they'll like that.

He answers, but through gritted teeth.

—How could you do it?

—. . . They've shot anyway. The lettuce.

—I said, how could you do it?? (*Silence*) I have just been to see the llamas.

—Ah.

—You couldn't leave him alone, could you?

—He barely felt a thing. The vet just nipped them off; it hardly took a second.

—You cut his balls off!!! You cut his bloody balls off, the poor sod.

—It couldn't go on; you know it couldn't. What would we have done with all those llamas?

—First you got to Hodge. And now I turn my back for two hours and you emasculate the only remaining four-legged creature in the house. If I'm not careful, I'll be next.

He leaves, slamming the door.

—Snip snip, dear! Snip snip.

◆

Oxford, Christmas 1962

Dear Kitty,

Guess who I met at a party the other day?? Dog Killer! DK! Of course he didn't recognize me, but I recognized him. He wasn't as cabbagey as the last time, but he had the same tank top (homemade, but by a better knitter than HQ—when I asked he said his sister had made it!). I went up to him and said hello and he looked at me a bit squiffily. I could tell he didn't quite have the courage to say he didn't know who I was, so I explained. "Your driving lesson. The dog." He got it then, and jokily said, "Oh yes, ill met by vomit."

It seems there's nothing better than sick to seal a friendship and we ended up stuck together for the rest of the evening—although that may be because I didn't know anyone else and neither did he. I can't say I have made many friends since I have been here. DK seems about as friendless as I am despite his being here for two years already, so we sat on the stairs outside the lavatory listening to the rustle of Bronco within. He mucked about with his pipe and I just looked at my hands. I asked him what he was studying and he looked at me as if that was a very silly question. He had a bit of the mad scientist look to him—with his long, lanky legs and untamed hair, I could imagine him bent over a test tube, in goggles and a lab coat setting things on fire. I said, "Chemistry?" but I was quite wrong there. He said darkly but firmly, "Philosophy." Then he lit his pipe, took a puff, and said "I'm Peter, by the way."

He said the dog had jumped out at him at the last minute. He didn't panic; he hadn't been frightened, just sorry for the dog. No one turned up to claim the bits, so in the end they wrapped it up in his overcoat and put it in the back of the car. I asked him what sort of a dog it was and he said, "A canine one." He never got his coat back and he'll never drive again. I said that was silly, you can't go through life without knowing how to drive, can you? He said, "What about you? Are you learning to drive?" Well, of course I'm not; why would I?

As I put my coat on, I said, "Maybe we'll see each other again?," but DK said, "Why?" and I suddenly thought that maybe I was being what HQ would call "too forward." That wasn't what I meant at all; I was just being polite. Oh, it's so easy to get things wrong. It would be better to stay quite silent and let other people be misunderstood for you.

I will be coming home for Christmas but, if I'm honest, I don't really want to. Life here is odd; it's not easy to get along. But, despite the high walls and the curfew, I feel so free. Back at home, I will have to deal with the boys and make mince pies and put holly on the mantelpiece and do all those things we do every year for no good reason but that everyone else is doing it. If anyone asks what I want as a present, tell them stockings, not books!

xxx

Oxford, early January 1963

Dear Kitty,

I feel like writing "back home at last" even though I have just come from what is supposed to be home. But oh, the freedom of my spartan room, the sash window that is still stuck, the staircase with the missing stair rod; it is bliss. HQ gave me some very bossy instructions as I left for the station; I must have tea next week with Louis something-or-other who is somebody's cousin or nephew. And she has written to him too (Louis whoever-he-is) telling him the same thing. We are to meet in the tearooms on the High next Thursday. Apparently, she met the parents in Antibes last summer. Or rather no, she met friends of the parents, and has now passed them on to me. It all sounds a bit vague and suspicious, but I don't see how I can wriggle my way out of it without being terribly rude. Why do parents think that their children will be interested in their friends' children? It makes no sense. You might as well expect two people to get on together just because they both have ginger hair. On the other hand, if they live in Antibes maybe I'll get a summer holiday out of it. There would certainly be better food and more sun in the South of France than there is here. As soon as I sat down on the train, I started to worry. What clothes do I have that would be suitable for the Riviera? What could I possibly wear? The answer: nothing except my shame.

So, next stop; Louis at the tearooms on the High. Will I have to speak French with him? We'll see (or On verra!).

xxx

PS. No news from DK, he must be in a sulk.

Oxford, late January 1963

Dear Kitty,

Louis was a surprise but not necessarily a disappointment. It's spelt Louis, but it's not Louis at all but Looey and he's American. If HQ had known that, she never would have told me to have tea with him. They don't live in the South of France but in America, so I can forget the summer holiday plan. There is a family connection in France and a house in Normandy, but I'll tell you more about that further on. The rest of the time they run what Looey called a laundry business in Philadelphia, but when I asked it turned out to be a row of washing machines with slots that people put money into. Of course that made me think of Toad, who disguised himself as a washerwoman. Then I saw the shiny car he turned up in . . . Gosh, it must be quite a big laundry with lots of machines whizzing around all the time. He really is Mr. Toad, poop poop!! But, dirty linen aside, he was charming—exactly the sort of person HQ would like us to marry—very comme il faut, steady income (clean money from dirty knickers), not too clever, no doubt good with horses. Not exactly a laugh a minute—but then he is American, so what do you expect?

He is over here for a year, sent by his parents to "soak up Europe"—or, as he said, to soak up Yurp. He is, it's true, like a great big sloppy sponge, tall and clean but empty. He says everything here is small, old, cramped, and uncomfortable. He was on his best behavior with me; I could see that he had been warned. He was about to complain about the tearooms (small, old, cramped, uncomfortable), but he changed "cold" into "cute" at the last minute, with a flashy smile that no one born in England would dare make. Even his car has a tooth-filled grin on the front.

Looey knows all his family history, from beginning to end and back to front, and he told me about it at great length. He proudly told me that his family had originally come from Shropshire. How odd to boast of coming from a different country from where you were brought up. His great-great-, or great-great-great-, grandfather emigrated in the nineteenth century. Now, listen to this bit, because this part was interesting, especially compared to all the rest of his family tree. There was a certain Joseph, a cousin of some sort, born late in the 1890s. According to Looey, Great- (Great-?) Cousin Joseph was in France in 1918 and fighting somewhere near Saint-Quentin. One evening they joined up with the British troops and they started talking, swapping cigarettes, chocolate, and so on. He met a lieutenant who said he came from somewhere in Shropshire and so of course they kept each other's names and addresses and promised to write after the war.

A couple of weeks later it was the armistice and Joseph was on leave in Paris. He met a French girl; they married, left Paris, and moved to the country, where her family ran a cheese factory. You see, this is where the house in Normandy comes in. He had kept the lieutenant's home address and he wrote to him but didn't get an answer for months. In the end, it was the mother, a Mrs. Owen, who answered; her boy had been killed in action, just a week before peace. She had put a postcard in the envelope along with her letter and there was a poem written on the back. She thought that Joseph would like to have it; her son Wilfred had sent it to her from France. Joseph never went back to America but stayed in France until he died, quite young, in the thirties. One of his distant cousins must have inherited the house.

Wilfred Owen, well! You don't get much better, do you? I couldn't stop thinking of the letter and that poem, sitting on a desk or in a shoebox under a bed. I asked Looey if Joseph had kept them, but he said he didn't know. Where was the house? Had he ever been there? He said it was a town called Vimoutiers but that no one had been there since the end of the war. The Americans bombed Vimoutiers to smithereens in '44 (yes, I do mean the Americans, not the RAF for once; they were busy bombing other bits of historic Europe) and Looey says there's probably just a pile of rubble left. But he can't complain—being bombed by his own, I mean. Anyway, I can forget about discovering a valuable manuscript and about my summer holidays.

Back to the chilly tearooms. He has a ridiculously flashy car, but when I asked him about it he said, "You know, I have a falcon back home," as if that was supposed to impress. "In an aviary?" I said, and he looked at me as if I was mad. Then smiled (more teeth) and said, "No, a Ford Falcon. Blue. It's a car, a convertible." I smiled (no visible teeth; we clearly don't have the same dentist). "Blue? How lovely." I expect his Mr. Toad car here has an impressive muscular, masculine name too, like the Vulture, or Tiger, or the Shark. Certainly not the Earthworm. Anyway, he may have a flashy car and flashy teeth, but he doesn't know how money works. He keeps saying "dollars" instead of "pounds," and he can't understand our perfectly sensible system. (Well, I have to defend it, don't I? Even if I did hate adding up all those columns at school.) I wrote it out on a piece of card for him to keep in his pocket. "Twelve pence = a shilling, twenty shillings = a pound."

When the girl at the tea shop asked him for tuppence ha'penny, he looked at me as I must have done when he said he had a Falcon. I explained what she meant, and he said, looking at the coins in his hand, "Well, why doesn't she just say that then?"

"Oh, but it's quite easy," I said—and I was a bit naughty, because he's right; we could just say what we mean, couldn't we?—"look, that one's a half crown, that's a tanner, that's a bob, and that one, that's my favorite, with the little wren on it, that's a farthing. And you can't have a guinea; they don't exist."

"So I have a Falcon at home, but here I only get a wren?"

Oh, Kitty, do you think he was trying to make a joke? You never know with Americans. I was going to make a remark about him having a "bird in the hand" but then thought it might be beyond him. Or that it might be a bit too forward.

When I got back, there was a note for me in my pigeonhole (yes, more birds) from, guess who . . . DK! What a fallen woman I am—only five months away from home and I already have two men at my feet. If only I could have chosen which two they were.

xxx

Oxford, February 1963

Dear Kitty,

I feel much better here now that I have Looey to look after. You see, he doesn't know anything at all—I don't think he really knew who Wilfred Owen was. He has a guidebook that he reads in the street (I mean, he reads it out aloud, to me!). We walked down Ship Street the other day and he looked up at some of that awful neo-Gothic stuff and said, "That's all just so old, I can't get my head around it." "Oh no," I said, "it's not old at all; that's all the horrid new stuff they built in the nineteenth century; they can't leave anything alone." And he said, "How can it be new if it's from the nineteenth century?"

Oxford is a bit like that; you are constantly buffeted around from one century to the next. It's all Gothic and then you turn the corner and it's back to the Norman Conquest; turn again and it's glass-fronted Woolworths and the pick and mix counter.

Have you noticed that I never tell you anything about what I'm actually doing here? What I am studying—or, as I now know we must say here, what I am reading. Well, I can tell anyone about all that. I want to talk to you about the things I can't tell anyone else. That is the point of you. So here goes.

Yesterday I got all tingly. You know what I mean I am sure.

Looey decided that we should go to the cinema together. He said West Side Story was on, as if I should have known what that was. Well, I didn't, and so we went. He picked me up in front of the porters' lodge (with old Mrs. So and So looking very disapproving when she saw the car) and drove to the Ritz in George Street and he parked right in front. I pretended not to be impressed, but of course I was—not by Looey, but the cinema. I'd never been inside before. Do you know, there's a café and a cloakroom, and you can't imagine how big the screen is; it's as if you were inside the film. Well, of course we both know what goes on in cinemas (as Kind Unk says—it doesn't matter if boys are boys, as long as we can rely on girls not being girls), and so there I was, with Looey, in the dark, and on the screen there were all these girls swishing around with their skirts in the air and kicking their legs up so high you could almost see—no, you could see—their knickers and I had this sort of tingly feeling, and if Looey had tried to kiss me I wouldn't have stopped him. I laughed and laughed and then I cried and cried—the music, the dancing, it all felt so new, so different. HQ would disapprove horribly.

At the end, the lights went up and Looey helped me on with my coat and drove me home and he sort of hovered over me as I got out of the car. I could see Mrs. So and So waiting in the lodge with an eye on the clock (it wasn't even nine, so she couldn't tell me off) and so I said thank you so much in my best Celia Johnson voice and went inside.

I lay down on my bed—I hadn't even taken off my shoes—and I could still hear "I like to be in A—me—ri—ca!" going on and on in my head. And those girls going round and round "A—me—ri—ca!" and again "A—me—ri—ca!" and Looey's teeth were flashing white in the corner of my eye and the girls were kicking their legs "A—me—ri—ca!" and still Looey was smiling and looking at me in the flickering light of the projector.

I woke up late, still all tingly, and when I went downstairs there was a note, but it was from DK, so I stuffed it in my pocket and went out. I forgot all about it and only read it when I got back tonight and was looking for my key. On the back of a postcard it said, in his careful italic hand: "Do you want to see the exhibition of Minoan pottery at the Ashmolean?" Signed "Peter." I thought I <u>should</u> want to, but I certainly <u>didn't</u> want to. I simply couldn't think of a polite way of saying no, so I didn't answer at all.

xxx

Oxford, March 1963

Dear Kitty,

I can't believe how stuffy you are. What do you mean, I should be more interested in Minoan pottery than American musicals? What is the point in being nineteen next month, out and about and free, if you can't choose not to go to see some broken bits of brown earthenware in a dusty glass case?

Looey is taking me to the cinema again tomorrow. This time it's David Niven and Gregory Peck killing Germans in the Mediterranean. One Englishman and one American, so we each have someone to cheer for. Not very Minoan pottery-esque at all, I can hear you say. Perhaps I might simply enjoy myself? And perhaps Looey might get as far as kissing me, or who-knows-what-else. (Yes, Mr. Tingles is back.) I have put on clean everything, just in case.

xxx

PS. Did you know that we are not allowed (we = women) to wear nylons for exams—unless they have a seam up the back! I don't know who could have thought up such a silly rule. Apparently, all those stockinged legs would be just too much for the men; their Great Minds wouldn't be able to concentrate on their Ancient History and might wander off into the treacherous realm of hosiery.

Oxford, May 1963

Dear Kitty,

It's hopeless, hopeless. I don't know what to do with Looey. I thought that our job was to protest and bashfully reject all those male advances, but he doesn't seem to know what an advance is, let alone how to make one. What more can I do, without being obvious, or too forward? (And, no, I am not going to say anything; that really would be too much.) As soon as I shifted over toward him in the cinema, he went all flappy and awkward (he who is usually so un-flappable, so un-awkward). Must I make all the moves?

Back home and there was another note from DK—he must have got the message about the pottery (or rather the lack of message in reply to), because this time he suggested we meet in the Parks, at the weekend. I instantly wrote a note to say YES (that'll show Looey). I will wear the frock from Barton's and I would like to wear my blue sandals, but they hurt my feet and it will probably rain, so my sensible browns would be more sensible (of course). I can't say they make my ankles look very attractive, which I have always thought were the most successful part of my body (compared to my dreadful upper arms that no-one in their right mind would be interested in). But sensible shoes and comfort it will be. DK won't look anyway. Or will he? He is so odd it's difficult to know.

xxx

Oxford, June 1963

Dear Kitty,

After all, it didn't matter about my sandals; we never made it to the Parks. I was right, it poured with rain, so we both agreed to put it off until after the summer and ended up in the Ashmolean after all. We looked at Uccello's The Hunt in the Forest, which is definitely my favorite picture there. (Oh, I have just thought! Uccello—in Italian, that's another bird. A Renaissance one to go along with all the other birds I seem to collect.) Uccello painted all those long-legged dogs rushing about and men in scarlet tights; you had to have good calves to carry that off.

"Why are they hunting at night?" I wondered out loud.

"What makes you think it's night?" he said.

"Well, because it's dark."

"What does that prove? It might be an eclipse."

Oh, that logical brain of his, how tiresome it is! Then in a sudden but brief moment of chattiness he told me about sitting under the kitchen table in his pajamas and dressing gown with his sister next to him, while the bombs dropped all around them. He has one up on me there. The Blitz; another thing I missed out on. I now begin to wonder if it is an advantage to have lived through the war. I mean, despite all its horror, it does give shape to one's life. A certain security in knowing what you have survived. Where you come from and where you might be going—I can't say that of myself.

It is the end of term and the end of year. Train home tomorrow; HQ said someone would meet me at the station and drive me back with my suitcase.

Summer holidays. I wish you were still there waiting for me; my room is so empty without you. There will be the usual house duties that HQ will drag me into, so there will be no time to write and nothing to say.

xxx

December

Scene III

In the dining room, Test Match Special *plays in the background. He is sitting at the dinner table, ear to the radio.*

She comes in from the kitchen, walking gingerly with a large tray loaded with plates, glasses, and cheese for lunch. She notices something on the floor.

—Oh, Hodge, really! *More* vomit! You could have gone outside. I thought cats were supposed to be naturally tidy.

He raises his head from the radio.

—That was Juno, not Hodge. And it's yesterday's vomit. Bright yellow.

She puts the tray down in front of him.

—I should get a sponge to it. But it's easier to wait until it's dry.

—Try what?

—Dry. (*louder*) I said, until it's dry. Haven't you put your ears in?

—Yes, I have. At least, I think I have. (*He puts one hand to his ear to check.*)

She points to the radio.

—Turn that off; it's lunch.

—It's not lunch in India.

—They don't have lunch in India. They have tiffin.

He turns off the radio.

—Pretty good. For England. Broad just took his third. Clean bowled him. (*He gets up.*) Right, I'll get the wine.

—Watch out for the cat sick.

—Ha, yes! (*leaving*) Stuart Broad's hat trick, excellent, excellent . . .

EXIT

◆

Breakfast. Mid-December.

Alice was with me this time; she had failed to find a decent excuse not to come. She rarely appeared for breakfast and sometimes only just for lunch, still pajamaed. She had finished school last year and was now studying chemistry in Paris; a quiet, methodical subject as far as possible from my world of the theater. She was in many ways, but not all, the opposite of me. To start with, she was French. Not half-French, half-English; all of both. Her father was from Brittany and liked to call himself a wildlife photographer. We met in Paris, spent an exhilarating week together, and then he suddenly packed a small rucksack and announced he was flying to Kenya. His plan was to travel through Tanzania and then on south to the Zambezi in time for the arrival of the carmine bee-eaters that migrated there for the winter months. As it turned out, barely a week later his own migration became permanent. A body was found floating by the greasy riverbank one morning. It took several days to identify and it was only when a hotelier nearby complained to the local police about an unpaid bill that they put two and two together. It seemed that he had fallen into the black folds of the river on his way home from one of the many bars selling cheap beer.

In the only photograph I had of him, black-and-white, he was walking along the canal in Paris. He was wearing an overcoat and the trees behind him were bare. He was looking down at something at his feet and the wind had caught his hair, half obscuring his face. When the news from Africa reached me, I had just discovered that he had left me with what was to become Alice. She would have no memory of him other than that photo that was now faded and curled at the corners. She grew up into someone pale, beguiling, and quite fatherless. Our losses were very different, but they also cemented us together in an unspoken way.

In the kitchen, Dad was making toast. A pair of tongs in one hand, he hung motionless over the toaster like a long-beaked heron, ready to dart in. Mum came in with a pile of books in one hand—books that I had lent them and she was giving back, or ones that she wanted to foist on me to read.

Birthday and Christmas presents from my parents were invariably books, mostly novels that they would read before wrapping. On opening you discovered a postcard stuck between two pages. A photo of a Greek vase or a slab of mosaic from Pompeii—on the other side the postmark gave an indication of how long they had had the book before passing it on. There were also presents (and therefore books) that we gave them. Charlotte's offerings were usually despised and left unread. (Mum: "Very kind of her, I'm sure. But really, I don't know what she was thinking . . .") Mine were given back to me with a review: "We didn't think much of that American one about the Spanish flu. Very faux naïf, we thought. Your father didn't even read it." Or, a double whammy: "Not funny or clever at all. The sort of thing your sister would enjoy."

Mum sat down and put the pile of volumes next to her. On the top, I noticed a small, mysterious item of clothing.

She picked up the butter dish and peered at it. "How did that get there?" With her knife, she scraped a dead bluebottle off the top and wiped it on the side of the table. "Did you sleep well?" I never sleep well in La Forgerie, but there is no point in saying so, and she didn't wait for an answer. "I dreamed of James. He's doing very well. He's learning to swim at the moment."

James. I must explain about James. He was a fictional child that we were often told about to show what bad daughters we both were. He always made the right choices in life—that is to say, the ones that Mum suggested. He would have chosen the shoes, not the purple jar. James's faultless progress in life had accompanied Mum's nights as long as we could remember. He was a card that she chose to play when she needed support in an argument (James was always on her side) or simply to fill a gap in the conversation. Charlotte and I had agreed that although the accounts of her dreams were probably true, she undoubtedly glossed over James's failures and only told us about his successes.

"He was doing breaststroke in the sea. He is a natural swimmer; you can see straightaway! A natural. He had a lovely knitted woollen swimming costume, the kind my father wore when we went to Guernsey on holiday. He came out of the water, all slippery like an otter. He had a fishing rod in one hand and a jam jar dangling from a loop of string in the other. I'm not sure where they came from; he couldn't have been swimming with them, could he? He was standing by a rock pool, looking at the seaweed, and he said, 'For what is sunk will hardly swim.' " She knitted her eyebrows. "Then the cats turned up and it all became very confused. 'For what is sunk will hardly swim . . . ,' what is that?"

"I don't know it," I said.

" 'For what is sunk will hardly swim.' Oh yes . . ." Mum's voice trailed off.

"I dreamed about work, as usual. I was onstage and had to understudy for someone, but I didn't know my lines and I was all tangled up in the curtains and couldn't get out. I suppose that's better than dreaming about my teeth falling out, which is my other option."

Mum turned to the books at her side. There was a doorstep-thick biography of Thomas Cromwell. She thought I might enjoy it, even if it was a bit long for me. I couldn't imagine there was that much to know about Cromwell, and certainly not that much that I wanted to know about him. I wasn't really sure who he was anyway.

Dad put the bread basket on the table just as Mum said, "Cromwell." He perked up. "Apple crumble? For dinner?"

"*Cromwell!*" shouted Mum. "Do *try* to listen."

"If I was blind and not deaf, you wouldn't make such fun of me."

"But you're not, and if you think it's fun for us, you're wrong."

"I haven't read the Cromwell yet," Dad said as he went back to his lookout position over the toaster.

"Yes, you have," countered Mum. "You enjoyed it. Here, Miranda, you can have *Wolf Hall* too if you want to know even more about Cromwell and Cardinal Wolsey."

"Oh, Hilary Mantel, yes." I thumbed through the book. "Another six or seven hundred pages of Tudors in tights, just what I wanted. Thank you." I swiveled round in my chair and looked at Dad. He was prodding at a piece of charred toast stuck in the jaws of the smoking toaster. "Have you read it?"

He shook his head, one finger in his ear. "My ears have just gone ping-pong; the battery must be dead."

Mum puffed out her cheeks and looked at the ceiling. "Oh for goodness' sake."

"Hilary Mantel," I repeated, louder this time, but he shook his head again.

He slung four pieces of blackened baguette into the bread basket and sat down. "There's no point in you two whispering, I can't hear."

I waved two fingers at him and mouthed, *Two words*, then opened and shut my hands like a book. *Author. Two words.*

If there was a game on, with the comfort of rules about how and when to win or lose, Dad would always make the auricular effort required to play. "Book! Ah, yes, an author. English or French? Stick your hand up for English." I put up a hand. "English, good. A chap or a lady? Right hand for a lady, left for a chap." I put up my right hand. "A lady, jolly good."

Dad liked games to be complicated—that is the point of them. Why do an easy crossword? You want the clues to be as cryptic as possible. So I stood up and started miming Hilary Mantel by making a pyramid shape with my fingertips touching. (Dad: "Chinese hat, no? Church roof? No?") And then making a much larger one. ("Mountain? Yes?") I stretched my arms wider. ("A bigger mountain? The Himalayas? Everest? Yes, good.") Then I mimed what was supposed to be a man walking uphill ("Skiing? Skipping? Morris dancers?"), and a heavy rucksack on his back ("Tortoise? Galápagos Islands?"). I gave up, sat down again, and let Mum take over. She started by pointing at the mantlepiece behind her ("Fire? No . . . Mirror? *Alice Through the Looking Glass*! Lewis Carroll wasn't a lady, was he?"); then she moved on to the title, biting and snarling like a wolf. ("Dragon? A lion? . . . *Born Free*!") Mum was now howling at the moon ("Pavarotti?"), but when she began to drool I thought we had had enough, and passed the book over to him.

He looked at the cover. "Oh, Hilary Mantel, I see. What was all that bit about Everest you did?"

"I was being Sir Edmund Hillary."

"Hillary, not bad, yes," he said. "But I would have done—" Here he stopped and mimed. He held up both hands, fingers spread— "*Ten.* And then—" He put one hand on his chest, the other held out in operatic splendor, and opened his mouth wide. "*Sing.* Tenzing Norgay. Perfectly obvious. And yes, I have read it." Then, nodding at the mysterious piece of clothing on top of the pile of books, "What's that?"

Mum picked it up and showed it to me. It was small, gray, and feltlike. "Now this, you may not recognize it, is your father's waistcoat. I gave it to him for his birthday, and it was rather expensive." It didn't look very expensive, but in particular it didn't seem big enough to contain Dad—it looked more like something designed for a large doll. Mum sighed and ran her hand down the woollen front. "He has spoiled it."

"Ha, yes," said Dad. "My waistcoat. Made of the finest barathea."

"Don't listen to him; he doesn't know what he's talking about. He wouldn't know barathea from a pig's ear."

"The pig would," said Dad.

"You see he can hear perfectly well when he wants to. He made a terrible mess eating his mussels; you know what he's like, so careless, he spilled them all down the front. The label said machine wash at thirty, so that's what I did, and look at it now!"

Dad stood up and started to fill the dishwasher, mumbling to himself, "Mussels? It wasn't mussels. We never have mussels. I like mussels. I'm always happy to eat a bivalve."

I looked more closely at the waistcoat that I was expected to pass judgment on. It was an often-repeated playlet. Mum would open hostilities by mentioning an object that has been broken or lost. The object in question was always good quality and/or a favorite of hers. If broken, it had been done so carelessly. If lost, it was because of Dad getting Alzheimery. She herself was never at fault.

"Are you sure you washed it at thirty?" I said.

"Of course I'm sure. And it *was* mussels. He's been very forgetful recently, although he won't admit it. Look at it; it's ruined. Things don't last the way they used to. Not anymore. It's the same with batteries. They don't last at all these days. You know that little alarm clock I have? It doesn't work as well as it used to; it loses five or ten minutes a day."

"Maybe it needs new batteries." I turned the waistcoat over and looked at the label. "When did you last change them?"

"That's the point I am making. They don't need changing; they still *work*. It's just that they don't work as well as they used to. Now, about your father's waistcoat. I want to go back to the shop; they'll have to give me a new one. I thought we could go this afternoon."

"Have you got the receipt?"

"Of course not; it was years ago."

"I thought it was Dad's birthday present?"

"Yes, but not necessarily this year."

I got up and went to make myself another cup of coffee. I would need it if I was to get through the day.

It was eventually decided that we would drive into Poitiers that afternoon. Mum would convince the shop to replace the waistcoat that my father had spoiled. "Decided that we would drive" meant that I would drive, in Mum's car, with her in the passenger seat giving advice. This was much better than the other option; her driving and me suffering in silence.

There had been no need for a car in Oxford; we walked or cycled everywhere, and if there were places that were too far to bicycle to it was generally agreed that we didn't want to go there. Neither of them had ever passed their driving test, but when they moved to La Forgerie they discovered that the French countryside was not nearly as conveniently laid out as the center of Oxford. I knew that many years ago Dad had once tried to pass the test but had failed. He had subsequently decided that he would never drive and he had rigidly stuck to that decision ever since.

Since it had to be her, Mum had learned to drive in Poitiers. She passed the test but wasn't a natural driver. She clung firmly to the wheel, her nose almost touching the windscreen, and could only go to places that provided easy parking. In Oxford, excursions had been limited by distance. In France, it was by the size of parking bays. On Saturday mornings, they drove into town to go to the market. Everyone else from the surrounding villages did the same thing and it was notoriously difficult to park. To avoid the problem Mum had decided that it was more enjoyable to leave the car just out of town and then walk half a mile along the main road to the market. This was called "stretching my legs."

She drove slowly and serenely in the middle of the road in second gear. Cars coming in the other direction might flash their lights and honk, but they always ended up swerving into the ditch at the last minute. As she passed she would toss her head and let out a, "Tut!" or a, "People just don't know their place." If I was in the passenger seat I would slump down, lower and lower, seeking invisibility. At the same time, I found myself making phantom gear changes or braking on nonexistent pedals with my feet. If, on the other hand, I was the one at the wheel and Mum was next to me she would offer useful instructions: "You'll want to go slowly here; there's a bend further on." Or, as I reversed into a parking space, "You won't be able to get in there! . . . Oh! How did you manage that?"

I had recently discovered one of her more bizarre driving techniques. I was the one at the wheel when she told me off for being too far away from the curb. "I think I'm fine where I am," I answered diplomatically. "Well then," Mum asked, "where are the windscreen wipers?" I wasn't sure what she meant—after all, where would they be other than on the windscreen? She explained that to be sure that I was in the right place on the road (if you are her, bang in the middle) I should keep the windscreen wipers lined up with the edge of the pavement. "Just keep one eye on that all the time and you'll know that you are where you should be." What happened, I wondered, when it rained?

———

Where were we? Breakfast and the waistcoat. I had just made myself another cup of coffee to survive the long day ahead.

On we go . . .

Just then, Alice came in, still in her pajamas and slippers. She had one hand over her sleepy eyes, shielding them from the glare of morning life. She slopped across the tiled floor, making a sound very similar to her grandfather. Was there anything more annoying, I wondered, than the sound of someone else walking in slippers? Sometimes I quite understood Mum's exasperation with Dad. From the same family of wading birds, Dad and Alice both had those long knobbly legs that looked as if they might bend backward at any moment. This morning her feathers were still ruffled, but her skin glowed like the inside of an oyster shell. To me she seemed beautiful but terrifyingly fragile.

Alice opened the fridge door, bent down, and looked inside. A tangle of long hair fell messily across her face as she stared blankly at the contents for a couple of minutes and then shut it again. "Isn't there anything to eat?" She stood up and noticed the red light on the coffee machine. "Who left that on?"

"Me," I said.

"Not very eco-friendly, Maman." And she flipped off the knob at the front *and* the switch at the back.

"No, I suppose not," I admitted. "So, Mum, where is this waistcoat shop?"

"I can't remember what it's called, but it's in the pedestrian bit, in the middle of Poitiers. I'll get the Yellow Pages." She leaned over to the dresser behind her and picked up the Pages Jaunes, as they are conveniently called in French.

"Don't bother; I'll find it quicker on my phone," I said as I swiped the screen. I had no idea that the Yellow Pages still existed.

Alice came over to the table and pointed at the waistcoat. "What's that?"

"Don't shuffle, Alice, or you'll turn into your grandfather. Ah, here it is!" Mum stabbed at the page with a finger. "Look, it's called 'L'Élégance Masculine.' " She glanced at Dad in his slippers and moth-eaten cardigan, a dirty cat bowl in one hand. "It doesn't sound very appropriate, does it?"

She passed the directory over to me. Past the pages devoted to gramophones, blunderbusses, and shooting sticks there was indeed a menswear section. I wondered which was older, the waistcoat or her edition of the Yellow Pages, but I had to admit that she had found it faster than me on my phone. So far, all I had come up with was a Google translation of waistcoat (*gilet*) and an online shop offering "seersucker shorts and premium leather deck shoes." I gave my phone to Alice and told her what we were up to. Before I had finished explaining, using just her thumbs and without glasses she had found the shop, the opening hours, and a map of how to get there. I showed Mum the screen.

"Oh yes, that's right; I told you so. Not far from the pedestrian bit, you see. I never go there. When I do my teaching, it's on the other side; I usually park on the Place de Gaulle."

She taught a group of what she called "My Old Ladies" who were in fact about the same age as her. She gave them English conversation classes, once a week. As she said, "They're never going to be able to actually speak English, but, you know, it keeps me on the go."

I was hoping to persuade Alice to come with us—she could navigate, to start with—but she claimed to have better things to do. She did, however, agree to set up the itinerary for us on my phone. Mum had never really got the hang of satnav, or how it worked. But then if I was honest, I hadn't either—I was just better at pretending I had. She imagined it as some sort of 1940s switchboard, with rows of Nice Girls in headphones and lipstick busily taking calls from lost drivers in Cowley

Bullnoses. "Turn right after the chemist, that's right, dear, and do be careful of Mrs. Prentice's dog on the corner," and so on. The first time she got into a car with me with a satnav, she listened to the voice and said, "Is it always the same lady?"

Dad had finished loading the dishwasher, shut its door, and shuffled across to me and Alice. He looked over my shoulder at the phone screen. "Amazing! How did you do that, Alice?"

I stretched out my arm to its maximum length and a bit more and then squinted. "We take the motorway and turn off just after . . ." Alice picked up my glasses and put them on my nose. I bent up my arm again and held the screen a comfortable two inches from my face. "Yes, it's the exit after the prison." I looked up to find Alice imitating me. She was goggling madly at an imaginary screen and typing with a single index finger. Dad looked at Alice, then me, and back again and shook his head, as if we were performing an intriguing but incomprehensible indigenous dance. I slid my finger across the screen and the map miraculously followed. "As I was saying. We turn off the motorway and then it's more or less straight on until the station, past Monoprix. We can park somewhere near there."

"The motorway? Oh no," said Mum, "I never go on the motorway; it's far too dangerous with all those lorries thundering along it. I always go the pretty way, round the back."

"It's slower going the pretty way, so you're not as likely to be killed outright," explained Dad, "but more likely to be severely and painfully maimed for life."

"Are you coming with us then?" I asked.

He looked at me with his steely blue eyes. "I would rather have red-hot needles inserted into my buttocks." He put a hand on the back door and said to Alice, “Come and see the pile of wood at the top of the field, would you? I want to get it in this afternoon, if you'll give me a hand with the tractor.”

Alice smiled and nodded at her grandfather.

“No one is coming with us?” I was met with silence. “Just you and me then, Mum. You'll have to hold the phone and tell me where to go.”

“You and your screens! What's wrong with a map?”

“Nothing's *wrong* with a map, but the screen is *better*. It shows you where to go.”

“So does the map.” I rolled my eyes and gnashed my teeth at the ceiling. Mum went on, “I have a very good little map in my handbag. Couldn't we use that?”

“Maybe you should ask James to take you? I am sure he would do a better job.” I held the phone out to her. “Look, you just follow the blue line. We turn after the prison, OK?”

Mum looked doubtfully at the screen. “There isn't a prison in Poitiers.”

“You can leave her there, if you don't kill her first,” muttered Dad as he opened the back door, put on his boots, and waved Alice out in front of him. “The blind leading the blind.”

From: MIRANDA
To: CHARLOTTE
Date: Saturday 08 December 2018 at 11:02
Subject: Arhggghhhh!!!

Christ! They are so insanely irritating!

From: CHARLOTTE
To: MIRANDA
Date: Saturday 08 December 2018 at 11:07
Subject: Re: Arhggghhhh!!!

What has happened? Give details please.

From: MIRANDA
To: CHARLOTTE
Date: Saturday 08 December 2018 at 11:31
Subject: Re: Re: Arhggghhhh!!!

Nothing spectacular. You know what it's like: the usual desire to kill . . .

From: CHARLOTTE
To: MIRANDA
Date: Saturday 08 December 2018 at 11:32
Subject: Re: Re: Re: Arhggghhhh!!!

While you're there, please make yourself useful:

1) The Incident; I want you to look in the photo album for a picture of Mum and Dad, Barbara and Sweetiepie. I am sure there is one—with woolly hats, out on a farm or somewhere. I can remember it. Maybe fur hats, not woolly.

2) Ask Dad about the uncle thing, from Aunt Bea. He hasn't answered my email. What a surprise.

Love, C.

PS. About the Hip, she has told me that she has fixed up an appointment with a doctor in Poitiers sometime in the New Year. Dad knows nothing about it (at least that is what she told me) and don't forget that you know nothing either!! Don't worry; I am dealing with it.

From: MIRANDA
To: CHARLOTTE
Date: Saturday 08 December 2018 at 11:41
Subject: Re: Re: Re: Re: Arhggghhhh!!!

1) Photo of Barbara: yes, will look after lunch.

2) Uncles: yes, will ask after lunch.

Love, Miranda

PS. Hip: No, I won't say anything, before or after lunch.

The Incident. Charlotte must have been twelve and so I would have been eight or nine. We used to fantasize about what had happened on that day, but what did we actually know? Ignorance of the facts was part of our small patch of common ground; the discussions that the not knowing engendered were one of the few things we could share. The Incident was never directly spoken about, only occasionally and obliquely referred to by Mum if she needed to trump Dad in an argument.

Barbara (never referred to by Mum as Barbara, only as "That Woman") had officially appeared on the horizon a couple of years before that. She taught philosophy at Princeton and her husband was a musician with the local orchestra. Dad had been invited to a conference in Boston and Mum had gone with him. At the end of the conference, they had stayed on in America. The four of them had spent a weekend on the family's farm in Sturbridge, an hour or so's drive from Boston. It didn't sound as if Dad had particularly enjoyed himself on the farm, but once they had flown back to England they had stayed in touch. Mum rigorously sent Christmas cards and Barbara the occasional letter in return. Several academic terms later it was Barbara's turn to come to England for a sabbatical year at Oxford and Mum had suggested—kindly but perhaps foolishly—that she stay with us in the spare bedroom at the top of the house.

Barbara must have been very clever, but she certainly didn't look like an Oxford academic. I can still picture her in a long, flowing, flowery kaftan, purple nail varnish, exotic earrings, and possibly a headscarf to tie back her unnaturally colorful mane of hair. There was a whiff of incense and Russian cigarettes about her. The husband, who had a beard but no name other than Sweetiepie, had stayed in Boston. Mum had been politely enthusiastic about her before she arrived but changed her opinion very quickly once Barbara was in the house.

In Boston, Mum and Dad had been the foreigners, the guests. They had adapted their behavior in consequence, as one should. She expected Barbara to do the same now that the situation was reversed. She should look up to the Lady of the House and welcome the advice she might be frugally but graciously given. Instead, she spent too much time in the bathroom, wore makeup in the daytime, and her hair! Well, yes, enough said. Barbara didn't believe in knowing her place and kowtowing. She chatted happily to anyone she met without looking up or down at them. She marched through her year in Oxford as if the place belonged to her, happily talking in dollars and swishing her bright hair. She went so far as to ask for a radiator in her room, a luxury unheard of for us. There was no heating in the house except in the dining room—a room that was only ever used if there were important guests for dinner. In winter, you got out of the bath and made a mad dash for your bed before the hoarfrost caught the hairs on your legs. Barbara politely asked if the heating could be turned on and said, jokingly, "You know, we Americans, we like our houses warmer than you do here. I guess that's what makes us warmer people." It was as if an iron curtain had gone down on Mum's face. A radiator was grudgingly supplied, but it still had a 1950s round-pin plug on it, so it can't have been much use.

On the spring afternoon in question we were in our room. On the same floor there was Mum and Dad's bedroom and a chilly lavatory that required expert handling of the chain to get the flush to go (a polite but firm tug). A steep staircase (no carpet) led from the bookcase-filled landing to Barbara's room on the floor above. We were sitting on the floor, secretly listening to Radio One (banned in the house), when we heard Barbara on the landing outside. Dad was there too; we could hear his low, understated voice but not his exact words. Then, suddenly, Barbara saying, "No, no no!" Then again, "Oh, Peter, no!" That made us giggle a bit because we had never heard anyone calling Dad by his first name and it felt intimate. Almost rude. We turned the radio down a notch and sat like mice. Dad had gone back downstairs by now, probably to make a phone call; we could just hear him talking in the hall below. Barbara was weeping on the other side of the bedroom door. Dad came back up again and murmured something that we didn't catch. Then we heard a door shut and a lock turn: he must have gone into the lavatory, because that was the only room with a bolt on the door. Barbara was still outside on the landing, on her own now. She was weeping and knocking on the lavatory door, but Dad didn't come out again. After a while, she gave up and went back upstairs to her own room.

Later that evening, after dinner (Dad had come out of the lavatory by this time, but Barbara had not made an appearance), there had been a major argument between Mum and Dad in their bedroom. Their door was open and we sat tight, our dressing gowns over our knees. We heard the phrase "That Woman" repeatedly used by Mum. Breakfast the next morning was strained and there was no sign of Barbara.

In the afternoon, when I came home from school, it was explained to us that there had been some fuss with her family. She had had to rush off back to Boston unexpectedly, before the end of term. I went quietly up the stairs to her room at the top; the bed was stripped to the bare mattress and the carpet had been viciously hoovered. All that remained was a stack of coins on the bedside table, some empty plastic bags from Blackwell's hanging on the peg behind the door, and the unplugged radiator standing in one corner. I slipped the pennies into my pocket and went out again.

Of course neither of us ever spoke about The Incident to Mum and Dad, but we did talk about it between the two of us. Even Alice knew the bare facts. We had, over the years, built up our own scenario, but we didn't agree on all the details. Charlotte was right about the photo album; I had a vague memory of a black-and-white photo of the three of them (not four; Sweetiepie must have been the photographer) somewhere on a windswept farm.

We were having coffee after lunch. Mum had, with great difficulty, lowered herself into the sofa next to me. Juno leapt nimbly up onto her lap. Dad was in his armchair and Hodge sat on the footstool by the unlit fire. Alice was nowhere to be seen.

"So then," asked Mum, "what are you up to at the moment?"

That was what Dad called a trick question—I could only get the answer wrong. If I said I had just signed a contract for a film, it would be bragging. If I mentioned an actor or director they had heard of, it would be labeled as name-dropping. On the other hand, if I said that I had no work, knew no one famous, and had no money, Mum would remind me that she had always said it was a mistake to want to be an actress. "Much better to have trained for a proper job. You could have done your acting later, once you were retired. Not of course that your sister did any better for herself . . ." I hadn't become a Hollywood star, but then I never wanted to. It was always the theater that had seduced me, the theater and all the absurdities of its ephemeral nature. Mum delighted in my failed auditions or bankrupt productions and even more so in my recent attempts to write. I was currently working on a production of *King Lear* that was to be staged in Paris in April. I had been cast as the Fool, but I was also involved in the adaptation itself, including a new translation into French. I weighed up my chances of getting the answer right and decided it was easiest to tell her the truth.

Mum awkwardly swiveled round to face me. "Why would you want to adapt *King Lear*? It's a perfectly good play already. And I don't see the point of doing Shakespeare in French. It's impossible to translate."

"Not impossible," I suggested, "difficult, maybe. And different, certainly."

"Similar," said Dad, from behind a screen of pipe smoke, "but not the same."

Mum marched on, without a glance at either of us, "No, not difficult. Pointless. And anyway, what do you know about Shakespeare?"

I looked down at the coffee cup in my lap. "I am the Fool too."

Mum raised her voice and hauled Dad into the debate. "Miranda is rewriting Shakespeare in French. What do you think of that?" He didn't answer—perhaps he hadn't heard? Or didn't want to hear. Mum went on, louder, "Shakespeare. *King Lear.* In French."

He heard that. "Jolly good. On the telly?"

"No, I told you. At the theater. Miranda is doing the adaptation. It doesn't sound like the sort of thing we would want to see, does it?"

"*King Lear*? Yes, of course we'll go. I won't hear it, but I'm still capable of seeing it. Unless someone gouges my eyes out before then."

The eye gouging was one of my favorite bits of *Lear* and I gleefully shouted, "Out, vile jelly! Where is thy lustre now?" with such theatrical vigor that Juno, who had been tidily tucked up like a roast chicken, was electrified into life and shot off out of the room, taking a large portion of Mum's knee with her.

Hodge was less impressed by Shakespeare and barely opened an eye as Dad pensively stroked between his ears. "Oh yes, vile jelly! I had forgotten all about that. When I was at school, we sometimes had a sort of gelatinous brown tapioca pudding for dinner that we all hated. We used to call it vole jelly. What witty little boys we were." He took a puff on his pipe. "*King Lear*, yes. I know most of it by heart, so it won't matter—if I can't hear, I mean. I'll see people with their mouths wagging and I'll know more or less what's going on."

Mum was disappointed by his enthusiasm and turned back to me. "Well then, aren't you Little Miss Shakespeare."

I swigged the rest of my coffee and stood up. "Right, let's go to Poitiers, shall we?"

I pulled Mum out of the sofa and sent her upstairs to find her coat and handbag. I leaned over the sofa to the bookcase behind and found the old photo album. I flicked quickly through the pages from back to front and then again from front to back but couldn't see Barbara anywhere. I slid the album back into place and stared at its spine for a minute or so. I did remember that photo, didn't I? Maybe I didn't; maybe I had got that wrong.

Never mind. Onward and forward with today's duties. I stood in front of Dad in his armchair, the shrunken waistcoat in my hand, and waved it at him. "We're off then."

"Ah, yes, I am sorry about that. It is my waistcoat and I have spoiled it."

I perched on the armrest next to him. "You should never have admitted to spoiling it; you could have just lied."

He tapped his pipe out on the edge of the ashtray. "As someone clever once said, 'No one is more hated than he who speaks the truth.' "

"Who said that?"

"I have no idea. But I expect you would like to ask, 'Herr Professor, can we know what *Truth* is?' "

"No, actually, I wasn't going to ask you that."

"I mean *Truth*, and not *The Truth*, of course. I don't think you can *know* what Truth is, but you can have an opinion. 'Somewhere between knowledge and ignorance, there lies opinion.' "

This reminded me of the uncles that Charlotte had nagged me about. She had dug up two different versions (not the same, but similar) of Dad's already very sparse family tree. She had sent him an email, asking him for an explanation. As usual, he hadn't answered. I had promised to ask, so I did. "Well then, speaking of truth, that reminds me. In between knowledge and ignorance, what's your *opinion* on your uncle? You know, the football one that Charlotte asked you about? What is the truth?"

"I have no idea where that absurd story came from. Well, actually, I do. Apparently, my sister came up with it."

Dad had an older sister called Bea. Mum used to say that we should be kind to her because "she was a bit slow," but I was never sure what this meant. She wasn't quite like us, I knew that much, but she was anything but slow. She was enthusiastic and industrious. "As busy as a Bee!" she used to say with a laugh. Mum and Dad laughed too, but not in the same way. Mum would put her hands on her hips, flap her elbows in a beelike way. "Oh yes, I'm as busy as a bee, dear!" and they both laughed, together for once. I liked bees, so what was funny about being as busy as one? Aunt Bea would sometimes appear for Dad's birthday in October, or later, for Christmas. She would sit and sew in the kitchen, never the sitting room, and she would make animals. Rabbits, foxes, bears, kangaroos. She stitched their bodies together, turned them the right way out, filled them with dried lentils, and then sewed up the opening down the tummy. Then she dipped into her sewing basket; there was colored embroidery thread for mouths, buttons for eyes, remnants of soft black leather for shiny noses or for paws. There were offcuts of muslin and lawn, lace trimmings and elastic for petticoats—because her rabbits always wore petticoats. She gave them names while she was sewing and brought them to life. Charlotte and I each had a rabbit, but what happened to the rest of them was a mystery—she had no family other than us. Perhaps she kept them all at home.

She had thick socks that were held up with elastic garters and thicker knees that stuck out over the top. There was something very woollen—but soft, not scratchy, perhaps beelike—about her. She sent us strange and exciting presents at Christmas: a music box with a pink ballerina inside, a set of black lacquer boxes one year, an ivory letter opener with elephants carved on the handle on another occasion. The origin of the curious objects often seemed suspiciously unbought to us—perhaps they had come free with Green Shield Stamps, or were family heirlooms out of a dusty trunk in the attic in the London house. Some years there was nothing, and no news.

Charlotte had recently been in touch with Aunt Bea and had started to ask about the past. She had developed a thirst for family trees and genetics that I found slightly disturbing. I don't think she was expecting to find a terrible family secret; she just wanted to know what came before her. She wanted to know about that layer of family that had already gone, disappeared before we had time to ask about them.

"This uncle thing," Dad went on. "She claims—I mean, *my* sister told *your* sister—that when we were little our father took us to a football match in Wembley and that we met someone there who was our uncle, and that we never saw him again. To start with, the idea of our father taking both of us to a football match is most improbable. He never took my sister anywhere, and he wasn't interested in sport at all. He watched *Pot Black* on the television—what he called 'the box'—but that's the closest he ever got to sport. He liked Fred Davis, but always said that Joe was the better player." I looked blankly at him. "Joe Davis. He was Fred's brother. Snooker. I like the idea of a sport that is played in a waistcoat and bow tie."

"So you don't remember meeting your uncle at Wembley?"

"Not at all. She must have dreamed up the whole thing. We didn't have an uncle. I mean, we had *an* uncle; he was married to Winifred, and they had a haberdashery shop. Or corsets, maybe it was corsets. She must mean that uncle."

"No," I said, "I saw Aunt Bea's email. This was a different uncle, an extra uncle."

Dad shook his head. "My father had one brother and one sister. My mother was an only child. Maybe you are thinking of your mother's uncle? What was his name? Edward or Edmund."

"Edward. And no, I am *not* thinking of Kind Unk. He was the one who gave you some money to buy the house. This is Aunt Bea. Your side of the family. She was quite clear. You never saw him again, after the football match. How could you have forgotten that? You didn't have *that* many uncles."

"I am quite sure we had only one uncle—the corset man—and an aunt who had little dogs and lived somewhere in Staffordshire. Or perhaps she had Staffordshires, and lived on the Isle of Dogs. We went to see her in the summer, in the Humber, which had shiny leather seats. Your thighs would get stuck to them. The garden was full of dogs, and dog turds. One time I showed off and did a somersault on the lawn—I'd just learned how to do them in Wolf Cubs. I got a dog turd caught in my hair. I couldn't have made that up, could I?"

"That's exactly the sort of thing you *would* make up. We'll never know how many uncles you really had; they are all dead and buried, so that's that."

"Does it really matter?"

"No, you're right; it doesn't matter." I could hear Mum clattering down the stairs. "It's just annoying to think that it's too late to know. That we never asked before."

Dad got up and we walked together to the hall. "David Vine, he was the presenter. *Pot Black*."

"David Vine? I thought he was Horse of the Year Show?" I said. "Anyway, that doesn't help with your uncles. Or with your waistcoat."

Mum was waiting for us by the front door, her hair clamped into place by a plastic tortoiseshell clip and her feet rammed into too-small town shoes. She looked at Dad. "Are you still here? I thought you were going to get the wood in, with Alice. It would be good for you; it would get you out a bit."

"We are just going now; I'm waiting for Alice." To prove it, he picked up his leather gardening gloves that he had put to dry on the hall radiator. "Shall I pick anything for dinner while we're out?"

"We'll have sprouts. I had a look this morning; they're rather good. Dear tight little knobs. I'll pick them when we're back. You always pick them too big, like cabbages."

"Well, they *are* cabbages really, aren't they?"

"Brassicas." Mum put on her coat, screwed on her rain hat, and went out to the garage.

I looked at Dad. "If all goes to plan and I don't kill her, we'll be back before it's dark. I'll do the wood with Alice, when we're back; don't worry. And no, I won't tell her."

"I had better do it. You never know."

When I was almost at the garage, I stopped and turned around. Dad was still there, hovering in the darkness, his gloves in one hand, watching us go. A line came to me from something long forgotten, I couldn't place it or say what came before or after: "By his dead smile I knew we stood in Hell."

◆

The car drove away. Alice put on her anorak and boots while her grandfather took the tractor keys off their hook by the back door and handed them to her. They looked out of the kitchen window and then at each other, then both put up their hoods. She couldn't picture her grandfather as someone to be feared. She was fond of him; they were similar in their silence. She put a finger through the key ring and together they walked to the garage.

She didn't recognize her grandparents when she listened to her mother and aunt. The two of them joked obsessively about them, always skirting around the heart of the question: their own glaring sisterly differences. She had no siblings to compare herself to, or to share parental attention—although if she believed the sisters, it was not parental attention they shared, but inattention. She found them cruel and pointlessly unforgiving at times. It was true they had been brought up in the swinging sixties and seventies as if it had still been the Victorian days, but they hadn't been beaten or starved. She had only one parent and she was an only child. She often wondered what it would be like to have a father—if not at home, at least alive, somewhere. When her mother worked, it was in the evening, so she found herself alone. But then her mother often didn't work; then they were together.

Her grandfather wasn't good with other humans—better with chickens, or trees. He didn't treat children as children—he treated them as adults or not at all. Now that she was older, had left school and gone to university, they shared something that helped not her, but him. He only did things that he could do very well, and then did them brilliantly. If he couldn't do something well enough, he simply didn't try to do it. Other people was one of those things.

She pulled the groundsheet off the garden tractor and trailer, sat down on the black plastic seat, and turned the key. The engine coughed twice and started, filling the garage with noise. No conversation would be possible until she stopped and turned off the ignition. Her grandfather waved her out, carefully shut the garage doors, making sure no cats were caught inside, and then overtook her again. He turned right and walked up the hill, holding up low branches for her and pointing out when there was an unexpected hole or ditch.

At the end of the laurels, they turned right again and up toward the tennis court, the trailer bumping along behind. Past the gate, they followed the hedge that separated the vegetable patch and the washing line from the top field. The rain dripped through the lime trees and plopped onto the llamas below. Her grandfather patted Lorenzo on his high, hard back and Leonora tossed her head as he slopped along in his boots next to the tractor. Alice parked carefully next to a large pile of logs that were stacked in one corner of the field.

"Excellent driving, well done," he said as she passed him the tractor keys. He put them in his trouser pocket. "I have put them in my trouser pocket. I am telling you just in case I forget before we need them again. Now we just have to hope that you don't forget that I've told you that."

She always thought it odd that someone so clever had been incapable of passing the simplest of tests. "You could drive the tractor, Grandpa, you know. It's easy, once you know what you're doing."

"I *do* drive the tractor, when you're not here. But I would rather you did it when you are." He pointed at the pile of wood. "Those are the logs I want to bring in."

"I'm learning at the moment, in Paris. To drive, I mean. On the road, in a car, it's much harder. You have to think about what other people are going to do."

"Exactly. Quite impossible for me." He picked up a log. "It should all fit in the trailer in one go, if we stack it carefully." He rubbed the oaky bark. "I did try, when I was an undergraduate. I had lessons. On the day of the exam, there was a dog in the middle of the road and I knocked it over. I killed it. So of course I failed."

"Poor dog. You could have taken the test again."

"Yes," he said, "I could have. But I have always been a firm believer of 'If at first you don't succeed, give up.' Here, have these." He passed her his huge leather gardening gloves that were like moose antlers on her.

"That's fine; you keep them." She passed them back. They began unstacking logs and piling them up again in the trailer. "You once gave me a very strange piece of advice. We were in a brasserie in Paris and you said, 'If someone takes you to a restaurant and you don't know what to order, choose the most expensive thing on the menu.' "

"What a wise grandfather I am."

The rain had stopped and they both paused, a log in hand. "You also said, 'Never eat Brussels sprouts,' which was far better advice." They put their hoods down and looked over the hedge at the vegetable patch. A neat row of Brussels sprouts stood, knobbly and windswept in the middle of the wintry earth.

"Yes, quite. Never eat sprouts." He thumped the log onto the growing pile in the trailer. "Sound advice indeed. If only all of life followed simple rules of that sort. I wouldn't get things wrong so often."

"Because life would be easier like that?"

"Absolutely. Clear rules and a scoring system, so you know where you are. You think that it might not work for everything in life? Not necessarily for everything in life, but for everything in *my* life, it would. You see, some people spend their lives inventing the zip, or nonstick frying pans, but Aristotle invented logic, which is much more useful. You know what logic is, don't you?" Alice half nodded, half shook her head. "How can I explain? Think of the crossword. The clues are cryptic, they are misleading on purpose, but even so they must follow certain rules. You don't know *which* rules to follow to find the solution, but once you have the answer, you can look back and check that there are rules to fit. You can be sure that you have . . . how could I put it? Made only legitimate moves."

"What sort of moves?"

"Legitimate. Ones that you are allowed to make."

"Oh, I see. Like an experiment in chemistry. You want life to be like chemistry, or like the crossword?"

"Yes, of course I do."

"But, Grandpa . . . Wouldn't we all end up doing the same things?"

"You mean that we would find the same results from our experiments, therefore have the same lives?"

"Yes."

"No, I don't think so. *You* know the rules to chemistry, but not everyone does. Not everyone can do the crossword. Or sometimes you think you can, but you put the wrong answers in. Knowing the rules doesn't mean you know which one to follow at a specific time to get to your destination.

You have to use your wit for that. You can know *how* to do the crossword, but still be completely stumped. But when at last you have solved the last clue, you can die happy leaving a full grid. 'And all things shall be well'—that's the first line of Aristotle's will."

"Was Aristotle good at the crossword?"

"Crosswords hadn't been invented then, but yes, I bet he would have been good at it; his brain was much better than mine. For example." He stood still, a log in his hands. "What about 'All Cs are B, all Bs are A, so all Cs are A'?" He looked questioningly at Alice. "Well, do you agree?" He added the log to the trailer.

"Err, well, what d'you mean?"

There was a minute of silence; then he went on, "Forget the As and Bs. What about this?: 'All my animals are chickens. All chickens can fly. Therefore all my animals can fly.' Makes sense, doesn't it? Unless I clip their wings."

"Yes . . . That sounds pretty obvious actually."

"Yes, but Aristotle could *prove* it. He could prove the bloody obvious; that's what made him so clever. 'If all llamas are animals, then every non-llama is a non-animal.' Or, 'If every chicken is not a llama, then every non-chicken is'—?"

"Every non-chicken is a . . . I mean, is *not* a . . . not a non-llama? OK, I get it. But it still sounds like garbage."

"Exactly, you've got it. Garbage, but *proven* garbage. Or you could say, 'If some Ds are C, all Cs are B, no Bs are A, then some Ds aren't A.' Now if life was as simple as that, I'd be on a roll."

"So," said Alice, "if I've got this right, 'all the wood is oak, all oak must be taken in, therefore all the wood must be taken in'?"

"Bugger, you're right. We'd better get a move on."

They chucked the last two logs into the trailer and Alice climbed up onto the tractor. She looked expectantly at her grandfather.

"What?" he asked.

She made a turning gesture with one hand. There was a moment of doubt in his eyes before he remembered and pulled the keys out of his pocket and passed them to her. She let the clutch out and circled neatly around the patch of flattened grass where the logs had been and then rolled back down the hill. He walked slowly behind her but stopped at the gate to the vegetable patch. The llamas had worked their way further along the hedge, nibbling as they went. He could still see poor, castrated Lorenzo silhouetted against the winter sky, his ears pricked up and his long neck craning at the leaves. He waved Alice on ahead and waited until she had turned left at the laurels and was out of sight. He leaned over the gate and with one easy, agile gesture he flicked up the catch and gently let the gate swing open an inch or so. Then he turned and trudged back down the hill.

◆

Oxford, October 1963

Dear Kitty,

There's lots to tell you but lots that I won't tell you. When I think, it's already my second year here! It has gone so fast. Term has started up again and so has DK. We finally made it to the Parks as we had planned in June, but it rained; now in

October it's clear skies and warm. I waited for him in front of hideous Keble as we had arranged and listened to the conkers dropping with a hard plop and bouncing off the pavement.

How can I describe it? It certainly wasn't an evening at the flicks with Looey. We walked to the pond and looked at the ducks. He didn't hold my hand or anything, just walked next to me. He must be two years older than me—he told me that he just avoided National Service and he's already in his last year—but he's no more grown-up or at ease with himself than I am. Then we walked again, right to the end where it's all bushy and unlooked after, and we sat on his coat (he has bought a new one since the dog-killing episode, a dusty mackintosh like old hydrangea leaves; he rustles as he walks). I sat on a spiky horse chestnut shell that split open under me. Two glossy conkers spilled out—I love it when there are two inside, each with one smooth, flat matching side. And the pure white membrane inside that you want to eat, even if it is supposed to be poisonous. I put them in my coat pocket and rolled them around in my hand.

Well, as we both know, as soon as you sit down on a coat with a Young Man, that's that; you have sinned. And it's true. I won't give you any of the finer details—not that they were very fine—but it was quicker and duller than I had thought. Talk of close your eyes and think of England—I didn't have time to shut my eyes.

Afterward, we were still on the mackintosh; he was lying on his back, his eyes closed (unlike mine), looking so pleased with himself. So . . . serene? Or more likely thinking about philosophy. I didn't feel serene at all. I felt all on my own, wide awake, and very ordinary. Nothing had changed for me.

I was just the same but dirtier, despite the mac. Disappointed, I suppose I was.

I didn't want him to be serene. I didn't want it to be as easy as that. I wanted to shake him up, so I said, "Did you know I call you DK?" He didn't move, so I shook him awake. "I said 'DK.' " He still didn't react. I prodded him in the ribs. " 'DK' for 'Dog Killer.' "

He opened his eyes and said, "You can't call me that; it sounds like 'decay.' You can't call me decay. But of course you don't have to call me anything." And he closed his eyes again.

What was I supposed to say to that? So I didn't, and neither did he.

xxx

PS. A note from Looey suggesting we drive out to see the Rollright Stones. No doubt he will have read up on it before we go and then tell me about it—it's like walking out with a Baedeker in clean socks. On the other hand, if we go in the car, I could wear my blue sandals . . . Not that this weather will last.

Oxford, November 1963

Dear Kitty,

A wonderful, soothing day out with Looey in Rollright. Did you know that one of the stone circles is called the Whispering Knights? Doesn't that sound beautifully romantic. Yes, Looey had read up about it and yes, he did tell me about it in chunks as if he was reading the encyclopedia at me. But he did it very nicely and politely (you would say boringly) and he did it sitting in the car, not on a damp mackintosh. He is so enthusiastic about the most mundane of things in life. ("Wow, just look at those quaint little streets!") It's ridiculous but comforting at the same time—I know more than he does, but that doesn't bother him as it would some people I could mention (but I won't mention them, and I don't need to; you know who I mean). He is so very normal, other than being American. Life together would be calm, collected, reassuring—although I am not sure what the laundry business involves. Maybe I would end up going round and round like one of his machines. Looey said that in America I could get my teeth seen to. I said, "What's wrong with them?" Then he smiled his big smile and I could see what he meant.

We drove back to Oxford as darkness fell and he dropped me off at the end of the road. I turned and waved goodbye and he drove off. As I walked home, I put a hand in my coat pocket and felt those two conkers from the Parks. I took them out and looked at them. They had been so shiny, so glowing, but now they were wrinkly and dull, so I put them in the bin. Things don't last, do they?

xxx

◆

It was almost dark as we drove down the motorway with lorries swooshing past us. Mum didn't like it if we went too fast and I could feel her tensing up next to me every time I changed lanes to overtake even the slowest of cars. At last I turned off the main road and up the drive to La Forgerie. As I parked and put on the hand brake, Alice opened the front door, a shaft of light spilling from behind her onto the gravel. She had been waiting for us. Had she perhaps been worried? I wondered.

We had spent almost an hour in L'Élégance Masculine and it had been excruciatingly embarrassing. But, as we went into the kitchen and Mum told Alice about the trip, I realized how differently she saw things. "To start with, your mother's telephone ran out of batteries before we even got there. It was lucky I had that map in my handbag or we would have been quite lost." Alice put a cup of tea in front of her grandmother. "Oh, thank you, Alice; how kind of you." She took a sip and went on, "Once we were in the shop, they really weren't very helpful; that place has gone downhill. They used to be such nice people. To start with I had a silly little girl, all thick makeup and a face like a spoon. She didn't even seem to know what a waistcoat was. Well, I made her call someone more au fait, and a rat-faced man in trainers duly scuttled in. Trainers, in a shop, can you imagine? He wasn't much better. 'I did exactly as the label said,' I explained, 'and look at the result!' He tried to tell me that I must have washed it too hot, and in any case there wasn't anything he could do about it. I wasn't having any of that, so I put my foot down. I made him call the manager, but a *woman* turned up and claimed that *she* was the manager. I didn't take any nonsense from her; I was polite but firm and in the end it was sorted out fairly quickly."

"What?" asked Alice. "They gave you a new waistcoat?"

"No, they gave me a voucher. For twenty-one euros."

"So what did you do with it?"

"I bought a new waistcoat of course. But don't tell your grandfather; it can be his Christmas present."

She put her car keys in the zipped-up back section of her purse and then put the purse in her handbag and handed it to Alice. "Put that in the back of the cleaning cupboard, would you?"

"Don't you think that's a bit excessive?" I asked.

"You never know. Not these days," said Mum.

She was right; you never know. Even so, it would have to be a very determined car thief—and one who collected twenty-three-year-old Peugeots with a sticky gearbox and only one wing mirror.

Mum washed her teacup in the sink and dried her hands on the tea towel. "Now I had better get going on dinner. Can you two do something about the potatoes? I'll put the oven on to warm up—they should go in fairly soon." Alice tipped the colander of potatoes into the sink, turned on the cold tap, and began scrubbing. "Thank you, Alice. The lamb won't need as long; it's a boned shoulder. I'll just go and get the washing in, not that it will be dry. I'll get the sprouts while I'm out."

"Sprouts! How lovely!" said Alice, as her hands swished around in the muddy sink.

We had washed, peeled, and parboiled the potatoes when Mum came back in from the garden, a plastic basket of damp washing on one hip. She slammed the door.

"That bloody beast!"

"What beast?" said Alice, looking up from the steaming colander.

Mum had found Lorenzo standing in the middle of the vegetable patch. He had slowly and methodically worked his way all along the row of Brussels sprouts. He hadn't eaten them all, only the tiny, new, tightly wrapped ones at the top of the stalks. He had scorned the bigger, cabbagey ones.

"That bloody beast! I could have sworn I shut the gate properly this morning. I'm ever so careful usually."

◆

Oxford, December 1963

Kitty!!

He has proposed!!

I have said yes!

Don't tell HQ!

I will, I promise; just give me time to think of how to tell her.

xxx

January

Oxford, January 1964

Dear Kitty,

A New Year.

I am going to tell you the truth now, because I haven't, not up to now. Well, not all of it. But you must absolutely promise not to tell HQ—not ever. Do you promise?? If you do promise, you may turn over the page and keep reading. If not, you can write "I don't promise" at the bottom of the page and post this letter back to me. Then I will know that you haven't read any further.

Write "I don't promise" here and send it back to me . . .

Oh, Kitty, you <u>have</u> promised; what a good sister you are; thank you for being here with me.

I had better tell you straightaway; then it will be done.

I didn't want to believe it at first. I tried not thinking about it, and not doing anything about it—I was sure it couldn't be true. I often miss a period and so to start with I really didn't believe it. I counted the days and put a tick in my diary and waited. Then I counted again and managed to convince myself that I had got it wrong, and added a couple more days on, but even after that it was no good.

This was all before Christmas, right back at the end of November. It feels like ages ago now; a different life, a different me. I didn't even have a doctor here; I'd never been ill before. You are the only person who I could have told and I couldn't even tell you; I wasn't brave enough. I was so ashamed. I know it's my fault and I should have been more careful as HQ would say—but what that actually means I'm not sure. How is one <u>careful</u>?

I didn't know what to do or who to ask, so I went to see Looey. He felt sort of neutral, and comforting in an outsider sort of way. I didn't tell him about the baby; it couldn't have been his anyway. I just wanted him to marry me. It seemed by far the best solution—he was in love with me; I was quite happy with him. I would have told him everything at the right time, whenever that was. To tell the truth I hadn't even thought that far ahead; I was just thinking about what to do right then. How not to be on my own. I would have told him if he had asked. At least I think I would have. In the end, I never needed to.

We met at the tearooms—the cramped ones that he always said were cozy, to please me. It really was cold sitting there that day. The Wild West Wind was blowing outside and I hadn't put a vest on. I knew that I would have to make the moves, he was so shy. I say shy, but I now think that maybe bland is the right word. He would never ask first. We sat cuddled up next to each other, in one of the booths with the brown leather seats, right at the back. My fingertips were pale blue when I took them out of my pockets. The waitress brought the teapot and the cups and I was about to say, "Shall I be Mother?" but stopped myself just in time. He put his usual three lumps of sugar in—you can see that he has never had a ration card—raised his cup, and said, "Cheers, old girl," in that silly English voice that he seems to think is funny. I laughed to please him and said, looking at him from under my lashes, "Don't you want to kiss me, Looey?" He spluttered over his tea and said straight off, "Hey, I love you loads, but I've got a girl back home. I'm going back next month to marry her. So it just wouldn't do if I kissed you, would it?"

It was as if he had thrown a brick into a lake.

All I could think of to say was, "No, it wouldn't do; it wouldn't do at all." All those months together, I had got him quite wrong. He had been lonely; he had been given my name by a friend of the family; I had kept him warm and happy until it was time to pack up and go home. I was nothing more and never had been.

He went on, "I couldn't possibly live here in Oxford, you know. I mean, you've got the greatest brains, but the worst food and the coldest houses." He is going back to Pennsylvania, or Philadelphia, whichever one it is; I always forget. He'll be much happier over there in the New World.

I didn't know what to do after that. I was quite alone with no one to ask, no one to help. I knew that there was something that could be done, something shameful and illegal. I had never thought of myself as a criminal; it almost made me laugh, it seemed so ridiculous. At school we used to whisper about that sort of thing, and what you could do. I knew that you could have a hot bath, drink bleach, move heavy furniture, or jump off a high wall, but all those options seemed just silly now. I did try pushing the bed in my room, but I hit my knee on the iron bedstead. That made me laugh. And then cry at the same time. Anyway, how would I know if it had worked? I knew that if you were really bad, you could go to see someone. But who? And where did you find them? I couldn't imagine how to begin to find out. I had a vague feeling that you asked the cleaning lady, but I didn't know one. I couldn't see myself going to a pub in Cowley and looking for a cleaning lady there. And if I did, what would I ask for? I didn't even know the right word.

I just had to tell someone, I felt so alone, and the only person left was DK, so I told him. I thought he would faint, or storm off and never speak to me again, but he did none of those things. He seemed a bit puzzled as to what to say. Stumped by a logic problem, or an anagram he couldn't solve. He filled his pipe and lit it—I could see his brain whirring away, so I didn't say anything while I waited—and then he took a puff and said, "Thou hast conquered me," which must be a quote from something. He is far better read (and far cleverer) than me and he knows it, so I smiled and said yes. I thought of it as "Thou hast conkered me," but when I put my hand in my pocket I remembered that I had put them in the bin on my way back from the Rollright Stones. That made me think of the Whispering Knights and Looey and West Side Story, and I was just about to cry when DK put down his pipe and said, "Well then. We had better get married."

I didn't expect that at all; I hadn't really expected anything. So I just said, "Oh, thank you," and then, "When?" And he said, "I'm going home next week, for Christmas. So in January? If that's what you want." And that was that. I can't say that I chose what happened—it just did. No doubt HQ would say, "You have made your bed; now you must lie in it." When I look back on it, it does feel rather odd—me going to Looey first and not DK. I can't explain it; we do funny things sometimes, don't we? After Christmas, we met at the tearooms and I could see that he had made an effort—he had brushed his hair, polished his shoes.

He is quite surprising sometimes; I never really know where I am with him.

We sat down at one of the round tables and he handed me an upright box; too big for jewelry, too small for a pair of shoes. It was leather, smooth as a holly leaf, with brass hinges and a little hook on one side. It was heavy, in a comforting way. I wasn't sure how to open it, so I looked at DK, and he nodded to the table. I pushed back the teapot and set down the box, gently eased up the hook, and the door swung open. Inside, nestled in dark green satin, was a beautiful carriage clock. Very plain. Brass with an enamel face and glass panels on the side so you could see the workings. I held it up to my ear and the ticking was as soft as a mouse's heartbeat.

He held out a small brass key and said, "It's yours now. Well, ours really. An engagement present." I didn't say anything. "It can stay in its box, if you don't like it." He said that with a dry laugh, as if it was a suggestion, not an apology.

"Oh no, no," I said, taking the key and turning it over in my hand. "It's beautiful. Thank you."

"Don't say thank you to me; it's from my father. He wanted us to have it and I couldn't say no. It was his father's, you see. My grandfather's. You have to wind it up once a week."

I turned it over in my hands and noticed a long and ugly crack down one side of the glass panel. "Oh, I didn't—at least, I don't think I did—I mean, I was ever so careful . . ."

"No, I know; don't worry. It has been like that for years. It's French, nineteenth century. You see those little bamboo-like pillars? That was very Henri Jacot."

"I didn't know you knew about clocks," I said.

"Well, I don't, not really. Just this one."

I tucked it back into its silky cocoon and as I shut the door it struck the hour. Not chimed; that would be too pretty a word for it. It struck the hour and my heart at the same time.

Well, now you know why we got married so quickly. It was only at the Registry Office; two witnesses and no guests or anything. No party and no dancing, I missed that.

I can't tell you much more about his family; he is very buttoned up about it. I know there is a sister, Beatrice, a bit older than him, still somewhere near London—Bushey Heath, it's called. He knows about the Hereford setup and rather dreads meeting HQ—but then everyone dreads their mother-in-law, don't they? He'll like the boys—at least, I hope he does. They can play tennis together, if the weather is any good and the grass is dry. They will have to teach him how to play croquet; he has never played (that's London boys for you—never seen the stars, too busy looking at the city lights). But croquet! Oh, those terrible arguments we got into! Me hiding in the woodshed in tears because I was so angry when someone had yet again sent my ball spinning into the hydrangeas. And HQ saying, as if it made the humiliation any more bearable, "Croquet is the cruelest game." We will have to go and visit at some point, who knows when.

Please don't say anything to anyone, not even Kind Unk. No one needs to know, not yet. Just give me time to sort things out in my head and then I'll write a proper letter. I will tell everyone soon—about the baby, I mean. I'll have to, because they'll see it, won't they? I'm sure I can feel her already. It seems very unfair, me having a baby so quickly and after just one go, but I'm sure it will be your turn soon. Perhaps I could lend you mine (baby, not husband)?

xxx

◆

From: MIRANDA
To: CHARLOTTE
Date: Saturday 12 January 2019 at 10:08
Subject: Hippos

A quick trip in between rehearsals with *King Lear*. Still no mention of when the Hip might happen. Or when the hap might hippen. Please tell Mum (if she asks) that she must get an appointment for the end of March or later as before that I will be stuck in Paris with *Lear*. I can't tell her this since I don't officially know about it, but I did make several loaded comments about being very busy in February and March and that I wouldn't be able to come and see them. Of course she will deny needing help or wanting us to come, but then be pissed off about us not coming to help. Grrrr.

After breakfast this morning, we had an exchange about fig chutney that you will enjoy. I don't really like figs at all, except those lovely black ones you get in Corsica, like drops of treacle hanging from the tree. The green ones that come off the tree in La Forgerie are floury and tasteless, so what is the point of picking them? Well, it turns out that the point of picking them is to make them into chutney, that is also floury and tasteless:

Mum: It's been a very good year for figs. I've made them into chutney.
Me: I don't like fig chutney.
Mum: James loves my fig chutney.
Me (*thinking to myself*): He would.
Mum: Lucian Freud used to make fig chutney. Of course he painted them too. Figs.
Me: I can't see why that should make me like figs. Or fig chutney.
Mum: You'll like *mine*. It goes with everything. Would you like a pot to take home with you tomorrow?

You will recognize the classic "Would you like a pot to take home?" line. Not a question, but a maternal command. I was sent into the larder to choose a pot. I took a chair with me to get to the top shelf, where I discovered hundreds of spidery jars. We laugh about the horseradish sauce, but you should see the top shelf! Any fruit that has ever grown on a tree in their garden in the last twenty years has been bottled or jammed, labeled, and never eaten. They don't even like plums and yet I counted at least twenty jars of them. (I asked Mum and she agreed that neither of them like plums, but thought that Dad might eat them when he was on his own!) The chutney section is particularly impressive.

Mum: Don't take a big pot; I haven't got that much and it goes very quickly. Didn't you read that Lucian Freud biography I gave you for your birthday?
Me (*standing on the chair*): Yes, but there weren't any figs in it, were there?
Mum: If you *had* read it, as you claim, you would certainly remember the bit about figs.
Me (*head in the spiderwebs*): I did read the Lucian Freud book, and I think you'll find it was quinces, not figs, that he painted and he made them into jam, not chutney. Here, I'll take this pot. It's not too big, is it?
Mum: No, but it's rather a pretty jar. You can take it, but make sure you bring it back when you've finished.

She was busily wrapping the pot in newspaper to keep it safe and since I had her cornered I thought I would ask her about The Incident. But when it came to actually saying something, to looking her in the eyes and saying, "What can you remember about Barbara? That woman with the scarves and the earrings?" I just couldn't do it. All I could come up with was, "Do you remember going to Boston?," to which she replied, "Boston? Oh, you mean America. I have always been disappointed by the Americans."

I'm not sure how we should interpret that—or if we should interpret it at all. She can't mean that she was disappointed by Barbara, can she?

About the Hip, please let me know when she has told you about the operation, and tell me if Dad knows, if Mum knows that Dad knows, and if I know officially or not.

Oh, it's all so maddening!!

Love,

Miranda.

From: CHARLOTTE
To: MIRANDA
Date: Saturday 12 January 2019 at 10:21
Subject: Re: Hippos

You don't have to go, you know.

From: MIRANDA
To: CHARLOTTE
Date: Saturday 12 January 2019 at 10:23
Subject: Re: Re: Hippos

Yes, I do. Just to make sure that one of them hasn't killed the other.

Oh, hang on. Dad's just come back in. We are off to play tennis—I will give you the score when I'm back.

It was mid-January, but we played tennis despite the frost and Mum's unmentionable hip. We always played tennis, whatever the weather, unless Mum decided that Dad didn't want to. And we always played in shorts and T-shirts, never long trousers and never a jumper. That would have been a sign of weakness. Dad always claimed that temperature didn't exist but was only a philosophical concept and therefore should be stood up to. The ducks, he said, didn't feel the cold because they didn't understand what it was—they had no concept of being cold.

It was just past ten and Mum and I were in the kitchen where she had been trying to foist some chutney on me. Dad came in from the garden, rubbing his hands together—so despite the cold only being a concept, it was a concept that he was aware of.

"I can only find seven ducks. I can't see Digory anywhere."

"Never mind Digory. Tennis first. Shall we play at eleven thirty?" asked Mum. The offer was accepted by Dad with a silent nod and he stumped up the stairs to get changed.

Mum turned to me. "Right, that gives us just over an hour. Take that chutney up to your room so you don't forget it tomorrow." She shut the larder door behind me and tidied the chair back under the kitchen table. "I want you to give me a hand with the creeper before tennis. Although I don't know why they call it a creeper, what with the way it races up the wall. I turn my back and it has got through the shutters and into the bathroom. Your father won't cut it back, however often I ask him. It's because he is too frightened to go up the ladder."

It was true that Dad wasn't a ladder man. He would happily chop wood, wrestle with brambles, or make giant bonfires, but he wouldn't do anything involving heights. "It's a good time to prune it, in the winter; otherwise there are so many leaves you can't see what you're doing, and it gets all twangled up with

Albertine." Albertine was Mum's favorite rose. It grew long and leggy all up the house, starting at the music room. On a hot June day the smell was almost too strong to sit outside.

We both went to change into our tennis gear and agreed to meet on the side of the house where the creeper grew, over by the duck house. Ten minutes later, now in my shorts and with January biting at my ankles, I dutifully went and got the ladder from the cellar and hauled it upright to stand against the bathroom shutters. I began to climb, a hoe in one hand to hoick at the furthest bits, a secateur in my shorts pocket. Mum stood below, her hair tied back and her wristbands on.

"Which bits do you want me to cut?" I called out. I pulled at a long, twisty section of vine and a large chunk of plasterwork crumbled away with it. I cut it off at the base, near the windowsill, and moved on to the next tentacle. As I pulled and cut, I threw the bits down to Mum, who stood below, one hand on the ladder, her legs firmly apart in her tennis skirt. If the ladder slipped, I thought, she could hang on all she wanted, but I would go toppling over. I clenched my buttocks and kept going.

She made a pile of the bare and broken vine at her feet. "Keep going; take it all down! It only grows back again."

"Are you sure?" I asked. "There's almost none left."

"Good!" Her face was turned up to me. She pointed. "That bit too, get that off."

I waved the hoe on my left and managed to hook it around the last remaining leg. The wall was now bare on the second floor. I came back down; we put the ladder away and went back around to the kitchen door.

Dad came out in his shorts and T-shirt, the tennis ball basket and three racquets under his arm. "Are you two ready? I've been waiting." He looked at Mum's hair that was full of vine debris and crumbs of plaster. "What have you been doing?"

"You haven't been waiting," said Mum. "You haven't even put your headband on yet." Dad went back inside to get his headband and Mum gave her hair a shake while his back was turned. She took the hoe out of my hand and put it behind the kitchen door. "No point in telling him now. It will have grown back before he notices."

All three of us trudged up the hill, past the vegetable patch, through the llama field. Dad kept an eye open for Digory, the missing duck. Past the old cherry tree, we stepped out onto the windswept plateau. There stood two llamas, both of them on the court, where, judging by the state of the tramlines, they had spent the night. Indeed, as we appeared, Leonora's tail rose and a batch of neat droppings, as shiny as black olives, rattled out and onto the court. Mum shooed the llamas back into the field and we knocked up. The usual formation was me against them—they played with the tramlines and me without. Lorenzo and Leonora now stood on the other side of the netting and were ambling toward the medlar tree that stood in one corner and where fallen fruit often lay late into the winter.

One of the golden rules of tennis was that I wasn't allowed to hit drop shots at Mum. It was also better to avoid her backhand and anything with topspin. What was required was a slow, smooth shot to her forehand, no further than a couple of feet from where she stood, but this was surprisingly difficult to achieve. The zone that Mum called "in" was a fluctuating area. Anything too far from her racquet was deemed to be unfair and therefore called out. Hit a serve too hard or with spin and it would certainly be long. To compensate, Dad liberally hit back any balls of mine that made it over the net. So in the end the score line probably more or less reflected reality.

Dad was serving for the second time when I began to notice that he was hitting all of his balls short and crosscourt. And then I realized why; his following serve was perfect. I raced up to the net and walloped it. As I did, I slid on a patch of frost, my legs buckled under me, and my racquet skidded away, clattering over the court. I rolled over, arms and legs splayed, and came to a slithering stop in the tramlines. The ball bounced three times, rolled slowly past me and off the court, then came to a standstill. I stood up; I was grazed and bleeding down one side and peppered all over with still-steaming llama dung.

"Ha! Forty–thirty!" Dad chortled with delight at his exploit as I picked up my racquet and plodded to my end of the court to await his next serve.

Despite his excrementally induced joy, Dad slowly sank into his usual tennis depression. He had been a decent but erratic grass court player when he was younger. With age he had slowed down and become even more erratic. He found this unbearable. The more points he lost, the harder he hit the balls. Harder and harder, and straight into the net.

At break point against him, he hit a giant ballooning shot skyward, that looped over the back netting and into the hedgerow behind. "Those were new balls!" Mum called out.

"Of course they *were* new balls. All tennis balls were new tennis balls at one point," said Dad, as he slashed at the nettles, looking for the lost ball. "Here." And he hit the ball back onto the court.

"Deuce!" called Mum—much to my surprise, since I thought I had won the game on the previous point.

Once I had won two sets all too quickly, we collected the remaining balls and went back to the house. I could see that going downhill was harder for Mum than up. On several occasions, she stopped to show me a gap in the hedge or to point out an early aconite in flower while she covertly caught her breath.

A thin drizzle was now falling and as we passed the laurels Dad called out, "Digory! Digory!" then, to himself more than anyone else, "Maybe he didn't come out of the house this morning . . ." He left Mum and me with the balls and racquets at the kitchen door and wandered off on his own toward the duck house.

"Oh, Digory! It's all he's interested in. Here, Miranda, put all the tennis stuff away in the corridor. I'll get the lunch things out."

"I'll just have a drink first." I turned on the tap, let the water run, and filled a glass. As I glugged away, the kitchen door opened and Dad came in. His mouth was thin and taut.

"I told you not to do that. I told you to leave it alone." He spoke through clenched teeth. He left the back door wide open, crossed the room, and went out the other side. I heard him climb the stairs to his room at the top.

"Oh dear," said Mum. "It's all very well saying leave it alone, but he's not the one who has to wrestle with the shutters when they are all jammed with creeper."

"Do you mean," I said, "that he expressly told you *not* to cut the creeper and that you made me do it anyway?"

"Well, not exactly. You see, the rule is that I can do what I want in the vegetable patch or the flower beds and he can do what he wants to the trees and shrubs. But the creeper is a bit of a no-man's-land. It grows in the flower bed, but it's true that it's not a vegetable and not a flower, is it?"

"I'm not playing Animal, Vegetable, or Mineral. I mean that you knew he didn't want you to cut it down and you did it anyway?"

"Well, yes, I suppose so. But he doesn't really know what he wants. I have to intervene sometimes or the whole house would be smothered in vegetation." She ran a glass of water for herself. "It was the same with Lorenzo. He was cross then and he'll be cross now. Three days, I expect, maybe a week."

And cross he was. I had forgotten what it was like. He came down to lunch with his hearing aid in one hand that he put on the table in front of him. A clear sign that he would neither speak nor listen. At the end of the meal, he silently stood up, picked up his plate, and went into the kitchen. Then, armed with his daisy fork and gardening gloves, he went out into the winter to attack the brambles. By midafternoon night was falling, but there was no sign of him. Only at six, his arms crisscrossed with scratches and his knees blue with cold, he came stumping back in, put the fork and his gloves on the kitchen table, and went upstairs to wash. Despite his anger, he still followed his own rules about changing for dinner; drinks, first course, second course, doing the ducks, cheese, and pudding. He simply did it all in complete, almost three-dimensional silence.

After dinner, he went straight up to bed and Mum and I were left to have coffee together.

Mum fingered through the collection of vinyl records on the shelf. "We might as well have some music." Mostly opera, but there was also a small section of more entertaining LPs. Songs by Tom Lehrer or Flanders and Swann. A few jazz classics, usually only listened to in Dad's absence. In his opinion, you couldn't go lower than jazz. She pulled out a dark red sleeve that I instantly recognized as Scott Joplin, "The Entertainer." "I don't see why we should suffer in silence." She put the record on the turntable and gently swung the needle across. There were a few crackles and then the piano opened with its cascade of jingling notes. She folded her arms and looked up through the ceiling to the bedroom above, and then at me. "I can barely hear it; can you?" And she turned up the volume, as high as it would go. I glanced at the empty carafe on the dining table, the slippery rugs, Mum's swollen and unsteady feet, and hoped that she wouldn't want to dance.

Instead, she went over to the mantelpiece and slowly wound up the brass carriage clock. She sighed. "He's not easy, Miranda. You don't realize what it's like. What it's *always* been like. He's not easy."

On Sunday morning at breakfast, Dad was still busy being silent. Mum made nervous small talk with me.

"You're getting the ten o'clock train, aren't you, Miranda?"

"Yes; it's the only one that runs now, unless I wait until dark." I looked at my watch. "I should make a move, I suppose."

"Don't forget your chutney."

"No, I won't."

Dad suddenly stood up, scraping his chair back over the tiles, and clumped off into the garden.

"I'll drop off the post when I drive you in." There was an impressive pile of letters on the kitchen table. "After Christmas, you know, I like to write and say thank you for the cards and so on." I flipped through the envelopes, all with handwritten addresses in Mum's neat, rounded hand. There were distant relations, a few friends in Oxford. And her two brothers, each in his own far-flung foreign country. I could see that she was trying to keep in touch. Trying to keep going.

"I'll just go and say goodbye to Dad."

"If you think there's any point, go on. He will have gone to poke his bonfire. He started it this morning, before breakfast. That's all he really enjoys—destruction."

I pulled on my boots and trudged across the lawn toward where I could see a thin column of smoke rising from behind the duck house. On the pond I counted all eight ducks safely bobbing. I could see Dad through the trees, standing next to a smoldering pile of creeper, a two-pronged pitchfork in one hand. His shoulders were slumped and he was wearing his tennis shorts but had wellies on his feet, displaying a stretch of thin knobbly knee in between the two. He stirred the fire and a plume of smoke rose and swirled around him, the flecks of white ash clinging to his hair and face.

He stood up straight when he saw me coming and waved the pitchfork, not aggressively, but not in a welcoming way either. Hodge was darting in and out of the undergrowth, looking for mice or bigger, but never straying far.

"Well, I'm off then," I said. Dad coughed but said nothing. "I'll be back next month."

He turned his back on me, skewered a pile of brambles, and tossed them on top of the flames. They gently hissed and crackled. He stabbed the pitchfork into the frosty ground next to him and went off again, ostensibly to collect some fallen branches further away. I stared at his back and then at the remains of the vine and noticed, underneath it all, something bright red. I pulled the pitchfork out of the ground and carefully poked at one side of the flames. There was something square and flat, clearly man-made. I flipped it over and discovered the molten remains of a vinyl disk and a record sleeve. Crimson with a black-and-white keyboard on one side. "The Entertainer."

◆

Oxford, February 1964

Dear Kitty,

Reality has suddenly broken in on me. We both have to move out of our rooms in college—of course we do, but I just hadn't thought about any of this until now. Everything has been exciting, or terrifying, or humiliating—or all three at the same time—and there has been no time to consider anything as ordinary as where we are going to live.

I sat down and chewed my fountain pen and finally wrote to Kind Unk telling him about my situation. Or perhaps, "my condition." He has come up trumps and given me £100 to get by on. No, don't tell HQ; she doesn't need to know. I can be sure that Kind Unk won't tell her either; I don't think there is much sibling connivance between them. He simply sent me a cheque with a little note paper-clipped to it that said: "Spend it! And not too wisely!" DK will be a junior fellow in October and that's £27 a week—enough to get by on—so it's just managing until then really.

We have found a flat to rent in Walton Well Road. I say a flat, but it's more like a room with a pantry at the back and basin attached. The landlady says I can park the pram downstairs (I haven't even got one yet) and there is a Baby Belling for cooking on and boiling up rubber teats, which is apparently what you have to do to them. The rent includes breakfast that she makes every morning if you want it, which I definitely don't—it's usually black pudding or liver. DK is going to have the back room, which is no more than a cupboard, but there's room for a desk, so he can work there. I have bought a notebook to do the accounts in, what comes in (that's easy, just one line) and then what goes out. You can't imagine the number of things you need for a baby, even before it has turned up.

I had to tell College about everything (they called it "The Situation") and they said I could take a year off and come back next Michaelmas term if I want to. Of course I want to; I'm not going to spend all my life washing nappies and boiling teats, am I? No one seems shocked or particularly interested about it all, but then they never do about anything here—unless it's the bypass or changing the rules about what color bow tie you must wear with your gown, and whether you must or mustn't wear the hood at the same time—honestly, it's like a playground full of horribly clever children.

I now go to a clinic which is supposed to look after me until the baby arrives. I am labeled an "expectant mother." We all sit around in a circle on brown plastic chairs and a chubby woman with thick ankles in a cardigan—I call her Marge, because that's what she looks like—tells us what we should eat and drink. For those too stupid to understand, she has a brown felt board and she pins cut-out pictures on it in two columns under a tick and a cross. She tells us that we must take iron pills and she puts this up on the board too: a picture of a bottle of pills and the days of the week in a list next to it, in case we don't know them. Then she leaves us to mull over what she has just said (she calls that letting it sink in) and the doctor sees us one by one. At least that bit isn't in front of everyone else. We feel a bit like naughty children waiting to see the headmaster. At least I do, and perhaps I am (a naughty child).

I know what you are thinking; I could have chosen otherwise. It depends what you mean by choose. It's true, I could have chosen not to lie down on the mackintosh in the first place (and yes, I chose to do so; I don't see anyone else as being responsible for that). But once that had happened, what path could I have gone down? You can't even be really sure that there is a baby, not to start with. The first time I went to the clinic, I thought that they would look inside, but they didn't. I asked Marge, "Can't the doctor do a test or something?" but all she said was, "A test? What for? You'll know soon enough, dear, when you find yourself hanging over the toilet bowl in the morning." Yes, she says "toilet," but that's the sort of person I mix with now.

Well, now I do know—I can see, and feel.

I told DK because I had to tell someone and there was no one else to tell. I hadn't really expected him to say, "Then we had better get married, hadn't we?" And I'm not sure that he expected to say that either; it just came out of his mouth. That's the done thing, isn't it? I could have chosen to say no, but I don't see where that would have got me. I would still have a baby but no husband to go with it.

Oxford, May 1964

Dear Kitty,

I was twenty last week. My second birthday in Oxford. Birthdays were always exciting at home; a rare moment when Pa and HQ were there with me, for me. An evening that was about me. That is all in the past now. I have become responsible for the birthday of someone else; it is no longer about me.

Another visit to the clinic this morning—they say you have to go every two weeks, but I'm not sure why or what for. It's a bit unnerving the way my stomach sticks out. None of my clothes fit me anymore except the most basic tent-shaped dresses. I don't want to wear anything fancy—I just want it to be over, but there are still weeks and weeks to go.

At the clinic, the doctor gives you an "examination" which basically seems to be him putting his hand up inside you (yes, he washes his hand first) and rummaging around as if he was looking for his keys. He takes your blood pressure and always says, "That seems to be fine, Mrs. Whatsit; you can get dressed again, thank you." What's he thanking me for, do you think? You put your knickers back on and out you go to Marge, who gives you a cup of sweet tea (she always puts the sugar in before you can say no). I said today that I hadn't felt her move as much as usual, but Marge said that was because there wasn't much room left and if the baby is comfortable it doesn't need to move. She got out a trumpet and listened to my tummy. "Sound asleep!" It means that she's in the right position.

Now I just have to wait.

Marge says we can come to what she calls natural childbirth classes. These happen in the same room, with the same people and the same brown chairs. I don't know if you can keep your knickers on for them, but in either case it is beyond my willpower to go. Marge says that it will help to deal with the pain on the day. I wonder what pain is like—I have never broken anything, never been ill other than whooping cough. The worst I can imagine is a beesting, but I presume that having a baby is worse.

I like to think of her as a real person; it all feels so surreal otherwise. She is a book I have written—all there, ready and waiting, but as yet unpublished. DK won't talk about "what happens when the baby comes," and if I ask he rushes off to the back room to read Plato. So I talk to myself about it, and to you. I am expected to knit baby clothes while I wait, and after a while I noticed that I had only made things in pink. I realized that I had always thought of her as a girl, right from the start. It will be funny if it's a boy after all that, but I suppose he could wear pink; why wouldn't he? That's what Victorian baby boys used to wear—pink—and girls were in blue. I have made a list of possible names, so that I am ready when she does pop out:

- Louise
- Susan (a bit dull, no?)
- Phoebe or Phyllis? (a bit obscure)
- Charlotte (like Great-Aunt Charlotte who had a bristly chin)
- Caroline

What do you think?

xxx

February

King Lear had opened on 2nd February for a six-week run. That meant that I was now stuck in Paris every week from Wednesday until after the Sunday matinée, which finished too late to get the last train to Poitiers. The show was draining—not just because it lasted two and a half hours but because it involved sharing a dressing room with the actress who played Regan. I had drawn the short straw. Last week she had cornered me before the performance, while doing her makeup. She had auditioned for a TV show and had just got a callback. She spouted on about how wonderful she had been in the audition, how dreadful the others were, and how sure she was that she would get the job. After what felt like an hour, she said, "Well, I mustn't go on about myself, must I?" She leaned into the mirror, opened her mouth, and drew a thick black line under one eye. "What about *you*?" She shut her mouth again and turned three-quarters to look at herself. "Do *you* think I'll get the part?" Actors rarely have many topics of conversation other than themselves, but Regan broke all records.

I still had no news on the Hip Front. Charlotte had sent me various links to health websites and had made lists of what must be done, or mustn't be done, when and why, before and after the operation. She went about it in many ways as if it was her own hip that was going to be sawn off and replaced, with gusto and an energy not shared by me. We were ready for the Big Push, but as yet no date had been set and I still didn't officially know of its existence.

Charlotte strove to keep our parents young. She wished that they would keep up appearances. I saw them more regularly and was quite willing to accept their inevitable decline. I did of course notice them slowly crumbling, like the house, but not as much as Charlotte did on her yearly visits, when she would point out the various ghastlinesses in a shocked voice. Had I seen the dead mice in the larder? The state of the lavatory upstairs? The horror, the horror! And what about that mole on Dad's back? Shouldn't he see a doctor about it? The growing layers of filth were invisible to me, as were the gray roots of Mum's hair and the diminishing number of teeth in Dad's mouth. If they couldn't be bothered to mend bits of their bodies, why should we tell them to do otherwise?

It was late on Monday afternoon and getting dark. I always tried to spend time with Dad in the garden where he could hear, although we didn't really converse; it was more Dad thinking aloud and me listening. Despite being a bookish academic, he was at his best in boots, thrashing about in the nettles with his pitchfork in one hand and his long hair swirling about while he tended the bonfire. Gandalf in wellies. He never cut down trees or pruned bushes but let them grow as they wanted. He only had two enemies in the garden: the brambles and, his Nemesis, a polecat that sometimes slunk in at night and had once slaughtered all his chickens. The animal had even been given a name—Nemo—in reference to both its status as an archenemy and its submarine movements.

We were putting on our boots and about to go and feed the chickens when Mum came into the kitchen.

"That was the Gendarmerie," said Mum. Dad clearly hadn't caught what she said. "The police! I was talking to the police. On the telephone."

Dad pulled on the first boot. "The police? What on earth did they want with you?"

"They didn't want anything with me; I wanted *them*. I told you, last night. I told you that I was going to call them. About Madeleine."

"Madeleine?" said Dad, halfway into the second boot. "Who is Madeleine?"

"You know, one of My Old Ladies. I told you." She looked at me. "I told your father last night, but he didn't listen. She's gone missing. I'm a bit worried; it's not like her."

"How do you know what is like her?" said Dad. "What do you know about her, other than that she's clearly never going to speak English?"

"Not at all. We get on very well together. Her husband is called Philippe. He runs a pet shop, so he can't be all bad."

"How do you know she's missing?" Dad stood up and stamped himself fully into his boots. "Maybe she's just run off with a taxidermist for a change."

I picked up the pot of vegetable peelings. "I expect she's fine, Mum; don't worry."

"She wasn't there last week. She always says if she's not coming. And yesterday, when I telephoned, she didn't answer."

"I think," said Dad, "that not answering the telephone is not necessarily a sign of something being catastrophically wrong." He put on his hat and opened the back door. "She might just be dead."

Along with the pot of peelings, we took a bucket of corn, a watering can to top up their water bowls, a bag of hay, and a rake to change the chickens' bed if they needed it. How did Dad manage on his own when I wasn't there?

There was a pile of red cabbage in the ice-cream pot along with the other cast-off vegetables. "There's no point in giving them that," he said, pointing at the cabbage. "They won't eat it. Even the llamas won't eat red cabbage, and how wise they are."

"In that case, why do you grow it, if you don't like it?"

"Of course we don't grow red cabbage; that would be ludicrous. We buy it. And you are quite wrong about me not liking it. I was recently told that in fact I am now quite fond of it. That is why we have it so often."

"Do you mean 'quite fond of it,' " I asked, "or 'quite happy to have it'? It's not the same thing."

"Quite different indeed. I am 'quite fond' of red cabbage, whereas I am only 'quite happy' with liver. I must have changed my mind about that at some point; I always hated liver. It was one of the few things that I was allowed to hate. But no longer . . ." He paused and threw some boiled potatoes through the netting at the chickens. "It's very kind of you to come. What my father would have called 'A and B the C of D.' "

"That sounds like an Aristotelian whatever-they're-called."

"Axiom? No. I mean A and B the C of D as in 'above and beyond the call of duty.' Which it is."

It certainly felt like A and B the C of D on some occasions. It was all very well Charlotte saying "you don't have to go there" from the other side of the Channel. I couldn't say that I *wanted* to go—perhaps the truth is that I wanted to want to go. Or to have been. It was the opposite of climbing a mountain, when you dread going up, but you're pleased when it's done and you're coming back down again. With La Forgerie, I was always optimistic before going and then, once I had been, fractious or depressed for days afterward.

I had my arm hooked through the handle of the corn bucket. "I just throw it through the netting at them, is that right?"

"Yes, five or six handfuls. Although if Zeno is right, they will never actually get the corn." Dad politely waited for me to ask him to explain, but I didn't, so he went on, "When you throw the corn, it first has to travel half of the distance from your hand to the ground. Then half the remaining distance, from that middle point to the ground, and then half again and so on. Dichotomy. And so on infinitely, there is always half of the half left that it still has to travel through. The corn can never hit the ground."

"Really?"

"Yes, it's quite impossible."

"Well, they're eating it, so it looks as if Zeno was wrong." I slid open the roof of the henhouse to see if there were any eggs.

"It may *look* like that, but that doesn't *prove* anything. You might *think* they were eating the seed, but your eyes are deceiving you. Or the seed might be *very near* the ground, but not actually on it, just hovering in midair. Remember the arrow and the rabbit? You think you can see the arrow sticking out of the rabbit, but it could be an optical illusion. Of course, the rabbit might not see things that way. You can't be sure. You can't *know*. The answer to a philosophical question is invariably yes *and* no . . ." He paused again, filling the hens' bowls from the watering can, pouring splashily through the netting. "At least I have Zeno to cheer me up. Things are unusually grim at the moment; I am back in the DH again."

"For any particular reason?"

"You don't need a reason to be in the Dog House. It is one thing to know that you are there, quite another to grasp the reason why. Perhaps it is because of her hip." I was about to say something but remembered just in time that I knew nothing about the matter. He picked up the sack of hay and turned toward the house. "Were there any eggs?" I held up the single egg that I had found nestling in the hay. "Only one? That will be my fault too, like the coffee machine. I expect you have been told about that." I nodded. "It isn't exactly broken; it's that she finds it difficult to fit the jigger into the whatnot. The fact that I can do it only makes matters worse. So we decided that it was broken—or rather, that I had broken it—and that we wanted a new one. Well, when I say 'we,' you know what I mean. I have always loathed that machine, but it turns out that I was wrong about that too; it was a Very Good Machine. At least it would have been if I hadn't broken it. So we bought the same one again." He chucked the red cabbage into the hedge as we turned and walked back.

"You couldn't buy the *same* one again. Surely you mean one that is similar?"

"Yes, sorry, how stupid of me. We bought a similar one. Which I can now loathe equally. I suppose it saves me thinking too much about the matter. I can move swiftly from one source of rage to another. It was a bad buy right from the start; it only lasted a year. In fact, it lasted exactly a year, to the day. When the guarantee ran out. They're clever bastards, these coffee people, aren't they? Still, it is only money down the drain, and as we philosophers like to ask, what is money for?"

"Spending?"

"Yes. And the more I spend now, the less the taxman will get when I die. And since I won't be around to enjoy the fact when I am dead, I am enjoying it now."

We had reached the back door by now and could see Mum in the kitchen. She opened the door for us, which was suspicious to start with. She was clearly in a bit of a state. Being in a bit of a state did not mean weeping or sobbing. It meant that her mouth was clamped shut in a straight line, but backstage you could see that things were a bit wobbly.

She said, as she held out a hand for the egg, "I told you so."

"I'm sure you did," said Dad, "but what?"

"I was right, it wasn't like her, not answering. The police called back. She's dead."

"Dead?" said Dad. "What, completely?"

Mum had been hoping for more. Perhaps not sympathy, but at least an acknowledgment that she had been right to worry.

"Oh, Mum, I am sorry," I said. "What happened?"

"I don't know; they didn't say . . ." There was a crack in her voice.

"The egg, Miranda," said Dad. "It's seventy-three." He held out a felt pen, which I took and wrote a wobbly seven and a three on the still-warm egg. They numbered every egg as it was laid. This was because Dad thought they should eat them in the right order.

"Never mind," said Mum. "One mustn't dwell on these things, must one?" She put the egg and the pen in the basket by the stove. "Yes, seventy-three. Quite right." She shook herself; her voice was brisk again. "The sun has gone down. I could do with a drink and a game of Scrabble. What about you two?"

That was what Dad would call a marital question—one that does not need answering. "Your usual?" he said, as he went into the larder to get the gin.

"And make it a large one. I'll set up the board!" called Mum as she left.

He put a tray out on the kitchen table. "Are you having the same? G and T?" I nodded. He put two tumblers and a wineglass on the tray. Now that she had gone, he was willing to admit what she had hoped for. "Goodness." He bent down in front of the fridge and put one hand into the icebox. "Your mother was right. It *wasn't* like her."

When Mum had told us about the phone call from the police, I had, at the time, found her tone triumphant. She had been right and Dad had been wrong. It was a victory to be savored. But now it seemed to me that she had been not coldly victorious, but in shock. Her hand had been shaking when I passed her the egg. There was that crack in her voice.

She hadn't planned this, hadn't been consulted. The fact had been sprung on her without her rubber-stamping the action. Of course Madeleine wasn't really a friend; she was an acquaintance, someone she had vaguely known for a few years and had always looked down on because she wasn't "our sort." But then Mum didn't have any real friends in France. In over twenty years she had made none, no one she could count on, or who counted on her, only those to be looked at from an angle, and mostly downward.

"What would you have done?" I asked Dad, as he took the ice tray out and began, with great difficulty, to prise out the cubes. "I mean, I bet you wouldn't have rung up the police, would you?" He shook his head and slung two cubes into each tumbler, on top of the gin I had already poured. "Imagine . . . What if Madeleine hadn't been dead, but lying on the bathroom floor in agony, both legs broken after falling over in the shower, and that calling the police had saved her life? I mean, what if I called here and you didn't answer? What do you think I should do?"

"Nothing." The lukewarm tonic fizzed and frothed over the ice.

"I might think, Dad is up in his room, at the top, working, without his ears in. Mum's in the garden planting leeks. She has had a heart attack, is screaming out for help, but you can't hear her. When I ring, no one answers. She might need saving."

"That depends on what you mean by *need*."

"Oh for goodness' sake! Dad! You're impossible." But he wouldn't look at me. He wouldn't be dragged into a conversation about anything he considered to be intimate. "If I called the police they might come and save her."

"Ha! It would be bloody lucky if you called just at that moment, wouldn't it?" he barked. "And anyway, if she had a heart attack, she wouldn't be screaming out for help. I suppose she might be gently wheezing."

"All right then. Say she was . . . bitten by a viper. She could still scream then?"

"Yes, but in that case the neighbors would hear. And if they didn't, the binmen would pick her up the next day." He pointed to a glossy prospectus that was sticking out of the fruit bowl between two overripe bananas. "Have you seen this absurd little brochure the *mairie* sent us about recycling?" I picked it up. "It has a list of everything in the world, and which color recycling bin you must put it in. Of course the thing that you actually want to throw away is never on the list." What sort of thing was he thinking of? I asked. "Well, for example . . . A dead hen. I looked, but it didn't say which bin I should put that in, so I put her on the bonfire. Her feathers went up a treat. And then on the back, look—" He leaned over, and showed me the other side of the brochure. "There." He pointed. "It tells you what they will be turned into. You look up 'underpants' and it says 'flip-flops.' Or 'coffee machine' and it says 'another bloody coffee machine.' And what if I want to throw away the brochure itself? It doesn't have that on the list. What about Madeleine? Which bin do you think they will put her in?"

"Lemon?" I asked, a knife in one hand. Dad nodded. "She did sound a bit . . . shocked. Mum, I mean. It's not really the done thing, just to go off and die like that, without warning, is it? No, she wasn't shocked; it's not that. Actually, she sounded upset—as upset as if it had been one of the cats. Certainly more upset than if it had been one of us."

"She'll cheer up pretty quickly; it will be something for her to do. Choosing a card, calling the other Old Ladies, organizing the outing to the funeral, making sandwiches. Who knows, I may even be able to creep out of the Dog House without anyone noticing."

"When we were little, *you* were the one who ran the Dog House. *You* were the one who was cross all the time. It was *you* we used to be frightened of."

"It was other people who made me angry. Now I'm just furious with myself."

I thought about his behavior last time I had come, when according to Mum he had only started speaking again a week later. "What about the creeper? You were cross with Mum and with me about that."

"No. I wasn't cross with *you*."

"You could have fooled me."

"Not at all. I was cross with myself for caring about such a futile thing as a creeper. I can't be bothered to be cross with other people, not anymore."

"Why not?"

"Ask your mother, if she's not too busy ordering a coffin. At least it's not for me. Not yet. It makes you think, though, doesn't it? One minute Madeleine was tooling along, not learning English, waiting for her husband to sell a budgerigar, and voomf! It's all over. If you believe Plato—and that's up to you—she's just gone off to be judged, or rather, not *her*, but her soul has. If you have been good, you get eternal bliss—whatever and wherever that is. But if you are guilty, you get sent back to earth, for another go. You might come back—at least, your soul would come back—in a different corporeal form. A dog, or a dandelion."

"You get recycled, you mean? Underpants to flip-flops?"

"Yes, though I don't know if Plato had a brochure to tell him which color bin your soul went in."

Dad picked up a glass, passed it to me, then took his own that he had filled with tepid white wine from the box and nodded to the garden. I followed him out into the dark. A single still-fizzing glass was left on the tray inside. The lights from the house spilled out onto the lawn, but there was no moonlight. It was damp and chilly as we gingerly made our way up the path to the statue of Bacchus that stood, moss covered and bird shitted, at the end. "Cheers." We both took a slurp.

"Now," Dad said. "I have something to tell you. Things are a good deal worse than I imagined."

"Worse?"

"Yes. She has suddenly announced that she is going to have her other hip done."

"Ah." I had trodden in something crunchy—probably a snail—and bent down to wipe the remains off my shoe.

"Yes. I thought you knew about that."

"That depends on what you mean by *know*."

"She has been unusually cordial since the creeper episode. I suspected that she was about to spring something on me. I asked her several times over the past few months if her hips were hurting, and I thought she always said, 'Of course not.' But apparently the true answer was, or rather would have been if I could hear it, 'Yes, like fuck.' She has already seen the quack in Poitiers, not that she told me when she went."

"She didn't tell me either," I said, quite truthfully for once.

"He's sharpening up his axe as we speak and the actual carving up will be in March."

"March?" Surely not March, I thought. "Do you know *when* in March?"

"No, I have no idea; she doesn't give me that sort of information."

"I hope it'll be at the end of the month, or I'll still be doing *Lear*. When she had the first hip done it wasn't too bad."

"Not too bad? Not too bad for *you*, maybe, in Paris. I live here."

We sat on the bench at the end of the path under the beech trees, too far from the house for the lights to distract us. In the mole-like blackness we could only guess where the other was from the chink of an ice cube. "Cheer up," I said. "You'll get a week on your own while she's in hospital. You can have oven chips every night and smoke in bed."

"Only a week? Couldn't you convince them to keep her longer? I'll pay whatever they ask." He was silent for a while. "How is your *King Lear* coming on?"

"It's going well. He's not exactly a laugh a minute, is he?"

"Dismal old bugger, if you ask me. A dismal dead bugger by the end."

"After all that drama and angst, when you get to the bit where Lear dies and he has Cordelia's body in his arms—"

" 'A plague upon you, murderers, traitors all,' " quoted Dad.

"Exactly. He does all that stuff—plagues and so on. And then it just says 'he dies.' Nothing else. As you would put it, voomf."

"Pleased to go I expect, after five acts. Ready for it. 'The readiness is all.' Do you remember when I died?"

Of course I hadn't forgotten the day that Dad had died. He had been in the sitting room, doing the crossword, when a wasp had flown in and got caught in his hair. He had swatted it away, but the wasp had got tangled even deeper and became understandably angry and alarmed. It stung him cruelly on the back of his neck and a few minutes later Dad started to feel unwell.

"You mean the wasp sting?" I said.

"Hornet, not wasp. I went out into the garden and lay down on the grass. It was dusk, and there was a red squirrel in the big hornbeam, just over my head. Then things went very hazy. I could still see, but it felt as if it wasn't really happening to me. 'Ah!' I thought to myself, 'the separation of soul and body.' I was no longer *empsuchos*."

"I'm glad, but hardly surprised, that you were thinking of Greek even in your dying moments and not about anything soppy like friends or family."

"I was quite sure that this was it, I was slipping away."

"*The Big Sleep*?" I said.

" 'You sleep the big sleep, kid,' " said Dad in his Humphrey Bogart voice. "No, death is not a sleep. The Greek for *cemetery* comes from the verb *keimai*. That doesn't mean to sleep, but just to lie down. So it means 'the place where you lie down.' The idea was that you lay there, twiddling your thumbs, waiting."

"So when the wasp stung you—sorry, the *hornet*—you were twiddling your thumbs, waiting for death. Were you frightened?"

"No, not frightened, just angry. I had things to do, unfinished business. I recall thinking that I had never had time to read *Middlemarch*. I don't know why that came to mind; it's not as if I ever really wanted to read *Middlemarch*. I hadn't set it as a goal in life. And I still haven't read it now. I was pretty miffed at dying, but not frightened. There's no point in being frightened of death. It makes sense to be frightened of *dying*, but not of death itself."

"Yes, that is all very logical. It makes sense, but we don't always say or feel what makes sense, do we?"

"Well, I do," said Dad. "You cease to exist once you're dead. Ashes to ashes. Nothing comes of nothing; you should know that. There's no point in worrying what will happen to you once the Grim Reaper has struck; it can't mean anything to you. 'Where Death is, I am not. Where I am, Death is not.' But you can worry now, in the present, about the future. About what will happen when you are dead. I can worry that the taxman will get all my money, or that my unread copy of *Middlemarch* will be thrown into a skip by my unloving daughters. And I can do something about that while I'm alive. I can make arrangements."

"So you could read *Middlemarch* now, throw it into a skip yourself, and then give me all your money. Then you would be ready for the Reaper."

"Yes, then I would have no unfinished business," said Dad.

"King Lear has no unfinished business. He makes arrangements. Stupid, vain, petty arrangements. He makes them in Act One and is incapable of changing them."

"Are you suggesting that I too am petty and vain?"

"No, just incapable of change. But Lear isn't a very good example of living in bliss, is he?"

"He certainly stops the taxman getting all his money—he gives it all to Goneril and Regan in the first scene. Although his daughters are no better than the Inland Revenue in the end. He would have been better off giving it all to the Donkey Rescue."

I thought of the last act and the death of Lear. The Fool had gone by then, out and into the storm. I could sit in darkness and watch from the wings every night. I didn't think Lear necessarily wanted to die; it was more as if he wanted to stop being. "It's as if he's had enough," I said. "That bit about him being stretched out on the rack of life. All that meaningless suffering."

"It's the same thing really—being ready to go, and having had enough. When the hornet stung me, I hadn't had enough. I wasn't ready."

"So basically what the great philosophers were saying is 'get everything sorted out before you keel over.' It's common sense really, isn't it?"

"Yes, I suppose that philosophy is a mix of pedantry and common sense."

I stood up and brushed a couple of beech leaves off his shoulder. I had just remembered the lonely gin and tonic that was still on the tray in the kitchen. "Come on. We have unfinished business. You haven't put the ducks to bed yet. And we promised to play Scrabble."

"Don't forget; you must let her make any words that she deems acceptable. And you are *not* to tell her that I told you about the Hip. She said she would tell you about it at dinner tonight. Remember to be surprised when she does. I have decided to call it Operation Fortitude."

"At least it will be inconvenient and expensive. That will cheer you up."

"It's kind of you to comfort me with that thought. But I see no light at the end of the tunnel. Except of course the Light of Death."

Going in through the back door, we topped up our glasses and put them back on the tray. Dad put a hand on my shoulder before we opened the door to the dining room. "That reminds me, in case we both suddenly kick the bucket. The bookcase in the corridor, on the top shelf. If you look inside *Lucky Jim*—it's a hardback, sort of bluish I think—there's five thousand euros in cash. You never know."

Mum looked up accusingly as we came in and so I made a rather thin excuse about not being able to find the tonic. I passed her her glass and noticed that there was already a long word set out on the board.

"I had to start without you." She had one hand in the bag of letters and was refilling her rack. "ZEUGMAS. Z on the double, that's twenty, plus nine for the rest . . . that makes twenty-nine, doubled, fifty-eight, plus fifty for going out . . ." She wrote down the score on a pad of paper at her elbow. "A hundred and eight. Your turn."

From: CHARLOTTE
To: MIRANDA
Date: Monday 18 February 2019 at 22:56
Subject: It's official!

I had an email from Mum to say that she has told Dad all about the Hip and that she was going to tell you tonight at dinner. So? Did she tell you?? Has she come clean and made it official? It will make things easier really. I won't have to lie about you not knowing. And you won't have to lie to Dad about not knowing about it anymore. Or to Mum about not knowing. Or about me having told you.

She sent me instructions that began: "Don't bother to come and see me, we can manage on our own, but if you do come, this is what you can do." Which makes it pretty clear that we are expected to come (I am taking her instructions as a plural "you"). I'm sure she would rather have James to look after her; I bet he has his scouts' badge for First Aid and would read Dickens to her in the evening while she reclines on a chaise longue. Hard cheese! She'll have to make do with what she has.

She's going in on Monday the 4th, and they actually operate the next day. She'll stay in the hospital for about a week, like last time. Although, remember, she was younger then. It won't be as easy this time. It's not a big op, but they'll need to keep an eye on her and give her physio for the first few days. One of us should be there, on the day, to sign the death certificate if something goes wrong. I mean hers, not ours. Or Dad's.

I can get some time off and come over, at least for part of the time. If you can come, it would be good—I don't mind driving in France, but I'm not that comfortable about it; I'd rather not if I can avoid it. Anything is better than Mum at the wheel. It won't be as bad if there are two of us, and at least we can laugh about the worst bits. And you could ask Alice if she can come with us. It would be a family outing!

Of course Dad will say that there is no point in us coming. That is his way of saying that I am interfering. If being interested in others and caring for them is interfering then yes, I suppose I am. There's not much we can actually *do,* but I was thinking it would be quite nice to see Dad on his own for once. We might even be able to have a conversation, or I could pick his brains about Barbara. Or he might prefer to sit in silence up at the top of the house and not talk to anyone. Despite what you say, I still think he is somewhere on the autism spectrum.

Love, C.

From: MIRANDA
To: CHARLOTTE
Date: Monday 18 February 2019 at 23:37
Subject: Re: It's official!

Yes, she officially told me about the Hip at dinner tonight and it is exceedingly inconvenient. I had carefully told her in January that *Lear* finished on the 17th and that I was free after that—I didn't say "so please get your hip done after the 17th" because I didn't officially know that she was going to have it done, but she could have worked it out on her own, I thought it would be obvious. Or perhaps it was obvious and she chose the 4th on purpose. Either way it is intensely irritating. On the other hand, it gives me a cast iron excuse not to come, except on Monday or Tuesday. Humph.

Here is an exchange from Scrabble:

Me: Would you allow KALASHNIKOV?
Mum: You can't make it, there aren't two Ks.
Dad: There's still a blank left in the bag.
Mum: No, there isn't. I have it on my rack. And anyway, even if she had the blank, KALASHNIKOV is too long.
Me: It was a hypothetical question. I just wondered if you would allow it.

Mum: KALASHNIKOV? Of course I would.
Me: OK. (*I put down UZI, getting rid of the Z that I had been stuck with for ages.*)
Mum: What is that supposed to mean?
Me: An Uzi, like a Kalashnikov. It's a kind of gun.
Mum (*in an end-of-argument voice*): Not one that *I* have heard of.

Today was complicated by one of Mum's Old Ladies dying. I don't think she was exactly fond of her, but she was definitely upset. She wanted to go to the funeral and was all revved up and ready, making a day of it. She was already making plans with the other Ladies—about sandwiches, looking for the thermos so she could take some hot Ribena, digging up an old stair carpet to use as a picnic rug, and so on. But during Scrabble one of them called back to say that the ceremony wasn't going to be in Poitiers but miles away, to the north. It turns out that Madeleine wasn't born near here at all but in somewhere called Lisieux. Her husband with the pet shop was the local one. The funeral was in the morning, so it was decided that they would leave the day before and spend the night in a hotel in Lisieux. They could visit the basilica, have a good dinner and plenty to drink and then a nice long sleep. The next day they would all go to the ceremony, have lunch and not too much to drink, then take their time driving back in the afternoon. Dad said, "Jolly good," but then he always does. After Scrabble (and for once she didn't win, so she must have been quite upset), we found the old red Michelin map and spread it open on the dining table. Mum put the sugar bowl on one corner and flattened out the folds with the back of her hand. The motorway went to Le Mans, then Alençon, neither of which are exactly tourist hot spots. "What happens after Alençon?" Mum asked. "Maybe there's a château or some gardens we could visit." She ran her finger along the red road and stopped at a little town just before Lisieux. "Oh, Vimoutiers!" and she sat down all of a sudden. "I once knew someone who had a house there. The family had something to do with Wilfred Owen, the war poet."

I said, "Why don't you drop in, see if they are still there?" Then she looked me in the eye and she said something a bit odd. I have put down exactly what she said:

"No. I will never go to that house. You must never go back. You must keep on the path you have chosen."

I could see that she was shaken, and not just by Madeleine; there was something else, something more distant. I was about to ask, "What do you mean? What path?," but she was already folding up the map. The moment had passed and I had said nothing. Maybe I was frightened of finding that she has emotions like the rest of us, under that shell.

By the time she had put the map away she had changed her mind and said she didn't want to go to Madeleine's funeral after all. It was too far and it would be tiring. It's true, Madeleine wasn't really a close friend, but even so.

I mean, there isn't anyone closer, is there?

Love,

Miranda

PS. As to Dad being on the autism spectrum, surely he must be on it, as we all are. Isn't that the definition of a spectrum, that it goes from one end to the other, zero to 100 percent? Otherwise it isn't really a spectrum at all.

I turned out the bedside light (I had brought a new bulb with me from Paris and secretly changed it last time I was there) and lay awake, bothered by the constant silence of the empty countryside. No police sirens, no binmen, no drunken screams in the street outside—the city noises that lulled me to sleep at home.

On my phone, I flicked with dissatisfaction through the news, looked at my emails again, and then sent Alice a message: "Can you come to La Forgerie on or around 3rd or 4th March??" She wouldn't be asleep and might just answer.

After a minute or so, my phone buzzed. "Must I?"

I answered, "Not mandatory. It would dull the pain for me."

"I'll think about it."

"Thx. Good night, Maman, xxx."

"xxx, A."

I turned off the phone and closed my eyes. The whole hip affair had felt comfortingly distant until this evening, but now, thinking about Charlotte's email, it loomed menacingly on the horizon. It was in fact next month; I had been so busy with the play that I hadn't noticed the weeks pass. Charlotte was right; making the trip down together wouldn't be as bad as going on her own—not for her. I could probably persuade Alice to come with us unless something else more exciting cropped up. I would have to go back to Paris in time for the first *Lear* of the week, which was on Wednesday. And that gave me an idea.

When we were little, Mum was the one who organized their evenings out. Mostly the opera or a concert, rarely the theater, once only the cinema (*A Bridge Too Far* at the Odeon).

When term started, they would sit down by the eternally unlit gas fire, each with a diary on their knee. Mum would read out her "suggestions" to Dad. The suggestions were not to be questioned. Dad would say, "Yes, jolly good," put the date in his diary, and then let Mum call for tickets. Just occasionally he would say something along the lines of, "No Strauss this year?" and Mum would answer, "Not one that you would enjoy." And that was that.

I knew that Dad used to go to the theater in London when he was a schoolboy, and that it was something that he enjoyed doing. Perhaps, I thought, if he was left on his own, he might want to come to see some Shakespeare. My idea was this: once Mum was safely in the hospital for the week, I would take Dad back with me to Paris to see *King Lear*. Charlotte would be happy to stay on her own for a day in La Forgerie and look after the animals. Dad could take the train back the day after and Charlotte would still have the rest of the week on her own with him. Mum would never know.

I thought of Mum not wanting to go to Madeleine's funeral. What she had said about the house in Vimoutiers. How could Wilfred Owen be connected to a town in Normandy? And who were these French friends she had never spoken of before? Suddenly two pieces of puzzle slotted together in my brain. That line came back to me: "And by his smile, I knew that sullen hall, by his dead smile I knew we stood in Hell." It was Wilfred Owen. The owl hooted and a distant dog barked. "By his dead smile I knew we stood in Hell." The line ran through my head again and again as I drifted into sleep.

The next morning I caught Dad out in the garden and told him more or less what Charlotte had said about coming in March. He was both surprised and, I was fairly sure, pleased to hear that we were coming. But he let nothing show.

"Both of you? And Alice? You really don't have to all come, you know. I can manage on my own."

"Do you mean that you would *rather* be on your own?"

He thought for a minute before answering. "I'm not quite sure what I mean. A bit of both, I suppose."

"I was wondering," I said, as we walked across the lawn, "do you want to come and see my *King Lear*? It's on until the middle of March."

"Me, going all the way to Paris, for pleasure?"

"We can have dinner after the show. I'll put you next to Cordelia; you'll like her."

"You'll have to warn her that I am a Deaf Old Fart. Perhaps she will think I am her father. 'But who is it that can tell me who I am?' " He laughed. "Of course, I don't know if I would be allowed; I'll have to think of a ruse."

All this nonsense about a ruse, of not being allowed to go, was just that—nonsense. Dad could do whatever he liked, but he found it useful to pretend that Mum wouldn't let him, so he didn't have to make difficult decisions on his own. A game of Who Wears the Trousers that they had played for so many years that it became reality. There was now nothing outside the game, nothing off the pitch. "It's not exactly that she won't let me go; it's more that the price of going is too high to make it worth it. When would it be?"

"Well," I said, carefully weighing my words, "I was thinking maybe the week of the fourth of March. If you see what I mean."

"Oh yes, I do." He thought some more. "I do see what you mean." I said nothing. "I could. I could go to Paris. On my own. . . . Well . . ."

"It would be quite safe." I found myself playing the game too.

"They'll keep her in for a week, you said?"

"Six days with good behavior. She would never know."

"All that palaver just for a leg. She doesn't even use it much. It's intensely irritating, but arguing about it with her is even more intensely irritating."

"A week's holiday on your own. And a trip to Paris."

"True. I promise to think about it." He turned to look back at the house. "No, I won't think about it; I'll say yes, now."

"Really?"

"Yes. Consider it done."

From: CHARLOTTE
To: MIRANDA
Date: Tuesday 19 February 2019 at 11:32
Subject: Hip Op / Nag list

Right then, here goes.

I have booked my flight and set out the following itinerary according to the information that everyone has supplied. You can print it up (and maybe send it on to Alice so she knows what's going on too?).

NB—Don't forget to read the notes at the bottom.

Sunday 3rd:

I land at 19h15 in Orly, not Charles de Gaulle.

You and Alice pick me up and we drive to La Forgerie.

We'll be too late for dinner—please provide sandwiches for the trip, no meat for me.

Let's hope they are not completely plastered by the time we arrive.

Monday 4th:

We leave Dad at home with Alice.

We drive Mum to the hospital, sign the papers, leave her there.

Dinner—maybe we could go out to a restaurant?

Tuesday 5th:

She has the operation!

Day off for the rest of us.

Wednesday 6th:

You drive back to Paris, taking Dad and Alice with you, and take Dad to the theater in the evening.

I have a nice day on my own—I can use the time to see if I can dig up any incriminating evidence about The Incident.

I do the ducks, have pasta and a hot bath, then go to bed early with a comforting book I have already read.

Thursday 7th:

Dad gets the train back again.

I can pick him up at the station with Mum's car—my driving abilities should get us that far.

Shopping if need be.

Visit Mum if that seems wise / desired / demanded.

Friday 8th:

Lovely day off.

Just Dad and me at home.

Saturday 9th:

Maybe Mum home???

How does she get back? Do I pick her up?

Or does the hospital provide transport?

Of course she might stay in longer, depending what the doctor says.

Sunday 10th:

I go to Paris on the train (NB must book a taxi to the station) and then fly from Orly.

How do I get from Montparnasse to Orly?*

Dad and Mum all alone at home in the evening.

*Sorry, stupid question; I will look at RATP website.

Monday 11th:

You go back to La Forgerie and check they are both still alive.

Notes:

- Tell Mum to pack a bag for the hospital; book / nightie / clean, presentable knickers / a toothbrush / iPod *and* the charger / mobile phone *and* the charger /

X-rays and medical file if she has it. What else?? We can always bring stuff she has forgotten when we go and see her.

- Tell Dad we will take him shopping, we won't eat the rubbish out of the freezer.
- Move the spare bed into the music room so she can sleep there and won't have to go up and down stairs.
- Remove all those slippery rugs.
- Can you ask Dad about dinner on Monday and book a suitable restaurant? The one on the river that does that revolting thing with catfish but that also has some edible food? He likes it there—mainly because the wine is cheap.

Love, C.

March

Sunday

Alice came to meet me at the stage door after the Sunday matinée. At the last minute, as I left my dressing room, I took a copy of the *King Lear* that had been published to coincide with the production. It had my French adaptation of the play, some color photos, and the director's note. I had been meaning to give it to Dad as a surprise when he was at the theater on Wednesday, but then I thought he would probably want to read it before coming since he wouldn't hear it on the day. I was rather pleased because the cover was a photo of Lear with the Fool clasped in his arms and, despite the makeup, I was recognizable. And of course it had my name on the front and down the spine.

We picked up a rental car and met Charlotte at Orly as she stepped out of the terminal. She looked smart as ever, her hair a careful ashy blond, cut straight just above the collar of her efficient jacket. The necklace was understated but expensive and came with matching earrings. She had a smooth black leather tote bag on one shoulder and a cashmere coat draped on the other arm. A small black suitcase trundled silently behind her.

As she leaned over to open the car door, her equally smooth hair fell in front of her face and she neatly flicked it back with one crooked finger behind her ear. I instinctively put one hand on the back of my neck and felt the nakedness, the simple coolness, of short hair. I wondered what it would be like to have hair that fell across your face, that you could run your hands through and toss.

There was always a settling-down moment with Charlotte when we met, face-to-face. We could happily chat by email, swapping parental anecdotes and horror stories. But when we actually saw each other, we were suddenly confronted by our unspoken differences. Mum said that Charlotte was ruthless, which was not meant to be flattering. Ladies, in Mum's opinion, should not intervene. They should look and listen. I would have called Charlotte determined or ambitious—perhaps that is what Mum meant by ruthless—but I would have meant it to be a compliment.

I had made meatless sandwiches as Charlotte had instructed and we ate them on the way there. I balanced mine in one hand on the steering wheel, with slices of tomato dropping out onto my lap. Charlotte nibbled hers neatly, like a squirrel with a nut in the passenger seat. Alice sat behind us, not eating. I could see her eagle eye in the rearview mirror, watching in silence. The blue glare of her phone lit up her chin and cheeks. The line of her jawbone, the way her hair fell and half hid her face; it was a glimpse of the past, of the photo by the canal in Paris. I briefly recognized her father in her.

"I talked to Aunt Bea last week," said Charlotte. "I thought I'd give her a ring and let her know I was going to see Dad. She's so kind, even if she is a bit dotty."

"She always was a bit." I wiped some mayonnaise off my chin. "Dotty."

"You can't say 'dotty' anymore, Maman," said Alice out of the dark from behind us.

Charlotte twisted around, the seat belt cutting into her neck. "We are too old to change what we say, Alice."

I raised my eyebrows and smiled at Alice in the mirror. "Definitely dotty," I said. Alice smiled back.

"Dotty or not," said Charlotte, "I told her what Dad said about the uncle thing, that he had no memory of it. And she now says that maybe, after all, the uncle in Wembley *was* the same as the haberdashery one. At least, she's not sure anymore. After all that research, I'm back to square one. One or two uncles, what do you think?"

"Either way," I said, "it's a very boring story."

"Of course, Dad might well be lying, just for the hell of it." She curled up one end of the bread and looked inside. "Did you use salted or unsalted butter?" And as she spoke the crooked finger came out and tucked away her hair again. It fell back in front of her eyes immediately. It was at moments like this that I remembered why we were never close. I kept looking at the road ahead, sucked my cheeks, and said nothing. Charlotte put her sandwich down. "You're right; it is a very boring story. I'll shut up about it now. But I have to think of something to write about to Aunt Bea. Since I do write to her." There was a tinge of the Samaritan in her voice.

"Yes, I know you make the effort to keep in touch with her and I don't." I sighed. "That is very noble and self-sacrificial of you."

"No, it's not. I like her. She's very . . . how could I put it?" Charlotte looked at me. "Trustworthy. Incapable of lying. Un-Dad-like. Don't you think?"

"I haven't seen her for twenty years. But I'm sure you're right." I licked another dribble of mayonnaise off my hand. "Not like Dad, that's for sure." I glanced at Charlotte. "Quite the opposite of her sibling, in fact."

Orly was behind us. We were on the motorway by now and I had the windscreen wipers going.

"Do you know," said Charlotte, "for a year or so, they were at the same school, in Bushey Heath. Dad and Bea. Every morning, they left home together and walked to the bus stop. But when they got there, Dad wouldn't let her take the same bus as him. He would get on the bus and make Aunt Bea stay all on her own and wait for the next one. She was four years older, but he didn't want to be seen with her."

"Do you mean, like a leper?"

"Yes. A bit like a leper. That's how he has always thought of her. Because she isn't clever."

"If I had been Aunt Bea," I said, "I would have got on the bus anyway."

"But you're *not* Aunt Bea; that's the point. Aunt Bea is obedient. And dotty—" She looked behind her at Alice, "I'm sorry, but I don't know what other word to use to describe Aunt Bea. That's what she is—obedient, old, and dotty. No, maybe not obedient. Kind. Doesn't want to upset people. I bet she didn't even think of getting on the bus." Charlotte folded up the foil from her sandwich and put it back in the bag. "But she still told me about it, sixty years later, so it clearly rankles. That was really cruel of Dad, wasn't it?"

"Oh, he was just being thoughtless." I had taken some apples along with the sandwiches, but no one ever eats the fruit you bring on a picnic, so I didn't even ask if they wanted one.

"No. You're always on his side. Being thoughtless isn't the same as being cruel. That was cruel."

"OK, you're right; it was thoughtlessly cruel. Casually cruel. Very like him." I scrunched up my foil into a ball and chucked it behind me, where it landed on the seat next to Alice. She gave me a look in the mirror that I interpreted as meaning "Don't you know that producing one ton of foil creates four tons of toxic waste?"

Charlotte took a notebook and pen out of her handbag. "We had better go through the plans for the week." She opened the notebook, put on her glasses, and clicked on the end of the ballpoint.

It was past eleven when we arrived. We found the front door unlocked and the house dark except for a puddle of light in the sitting room. Dad was in his armchair, swathed in pipe smoke and a book open, his glasses on a string around his neck but with his eyes closed. Hodge was rolled in a tight ball on his knees, his eyes no more than green slits. Alice waved a silent hand at us and sped up the stairs to her room.

Dad woke up as we came in and Hodge uncoiled himself. They both came over to the dining table, where Dad had put out some cheese and a carafe. He poured us each a large glass of box wine that neither of us really wanted but both felt we ought to have. He had clearly already had several glasses of his own. When it came to wine, he thought quantity was more important than quality. If he asked you what wine you wanted, the answer wasn't Bordeaux or Burgundy but red or white.

"Where's Alice? Didn't she come with you?" he asked. "I was looking forward to seeing her."

"Yes, she did, but she went straight up. She didn't want to wake you."

"But *we* are here, Dad," said Charlotte, slightly miffed. "Has Mum gone to bed then?"

"Bed? Oh no, she's gone. I mean completely. She left this afternoon."

It turned out that the hospital had called on Friday. The operation had been moved not backward but forward—to tomorrow, Monday, instead of Tuesday. Mum had taken a taxi to Poitiers that afternoon, but neither of them had thought to warn us. As Dad said, what difference did it make, us knowing or not? We would have come anyway. He was right, it made little or no difference, but Charlotte didn't like having her plans changed. I was used to it; that was what happened every night at the theater. It was absurd to think that onstage, or in real life, everyone would say all of their lines in the right order. That technicians would set off explosions when they were expected, or costume changes would happen as planned at lightning speed in the wings. Every night there was a minor catastrophe backstage with people silently cursing but not panicking, putting safety pins down the back of a doublet or rewiring a smoke machine in the dark. Onstage all was smooth perfection; a glossy mandarin duck floating on a ripple-free lake while, under the surface, its webs were paddling like fury to keep everything afloat. All that was certain was that the curtain must go up and at some point it would come down again. In between the two, whatever happened, you had to keep going.

"It makes no difference to me," said Dad. "Does it, Charlotte?"

"You shouldn't let them push you around."

"I *didn't* let them push me around." Dad waved a hand, swatting the matter away. "I don't care."

"Well, I do," said Charlotte. "These people at the hospital, they work for *you*, not you for them." I could see the ruthless glint in her eye. She opened her tote bag and took out a sheaf of French paperwork that she started sifting through. "It's lucky I printed this all up before leaving home." The crooked finger came out and flicked the hair back behind her ear. She was indignant. How could the hospital be so badly organized? It wouldn't happen in England; they would have consulted the family first! It isn't good enough! We should make a formal complaint! She had already found the name of the hospital administrator in the paperwork that she had spread out on the table. "We mustn't let them get away with it; it's disgraceful."

"*I* am quite happy for them to get away with it," I said. "*You* can do something if you want. Surely there are more interesting battles to be fought?"

But not for Charlotte, and we went to bed with a certain coolness hanging over us.

Monday

Monday was a glorious, bluebell-filled March day, one of those spring days that make you think it is almost summer. After lunch, I sat out in the garden with Charlotte. Alice was upstairs and Dad snoozed inside. We were all waiting for Mum to call with news of how the operation had gone that morning. We couldn't call her because, although she did have the mobile phone that we had given her, and that she had taken with her following Charlotte's strict instructions, she hadn't actually turned it on. The charger that went with it was sitting in the basket on the table in the hall and seemed to exude an aura of having been forgotten on purpose.

We had moved the garden table onto the lawn. Like Boswell, the table had started its life a deep chocolate color, but the teak had been bleached dry by years of sun. It spent the winter months in the *buanderie* along with the new freezer and the bats that nested above. Charlotte had taken a bucket of warm water and a brush that she had found under the stairs and was briskly scrubbing.

I rang the restaurant to book for the evening and discovered that they were full. I knew I should have called them last week and now I had no choice but to own up to my failing to Charlotte. "It's Monday," I said. "They're shut. For dinner tonight I'll drive into Poitiers and get something there." Charlotte was still silently and furiously scrubbing. She hadn't forgiven me yet for not agreeing with her last night. "I don't know why you bother cleaning it. It's their table; if they like it like that, all covered in bat shit, then let them have it."

She stepped back to evaluate the result. "It gets worse every time I come."

"Well, think of me, and how often I come!"

"You don't have to," she said between gritted teeth.

"Yes, I know I don't *have* to. But I *do*." I was joking, but Charlotte was deadly serious.

"You're just as bad as them. You just let things wash over you as if nothing mattered. You make no attempt to change the course of things." She angrily shook the excess water off the scrubbing brush into the flower bed. "You're so fucking complacent. That's why you were always the favorite one."

I didn't know what to say to that. Was there a favorite one? Surely we were equally scorned.

Charlotte went on, "You'd never thought of that, had you, that you were the favorite one? And that proves it. You don't notice, if you *are* the favorite one. It's the unfavorite one who notices. You were the one they wanted; I was the mistake!"

"Oh, but I don't think—"

But Charlotte was unstoppable now that she had started. "No, you wouldn't think, would you? It was because of me that Mum never finished her degree. That's why she didn't want me to go to university, so that I wouldn't do any better than she did!" I tried to say something, but she pointed the brush at my face, the soapy water dripping down her hand and along her arm. She was so close I could see that she wasn't joking. "Let me say this. I am going to say it. I was the one called Charlotte, named after Great-Aunt Charlotte with the bristly chin! I was the one who was sent away on my own to stay with a pen friend in France I had never even met! A whole month! I was the one they abandoned, left in England, when they moved to France." She ran a wet dishcloth over the tabletop. "That will have to do; I can't get it any better." She tipped the gray water out of the bucket onto the flower bed and sat down. "You see? They followed *you*, just when you thought you had escaped. That is your punishment."

I thought this was quite illogical of her. Either she had been abandoned and I was blessed by their presence. Or she was blessed by them leaving and I was punished by their presence. She couldn't have it both ways.

"Here, have one of these." I held up my pack of Camels, but she swatted them away. "If it's any comfort, I was jealous of you, having that summer with your pen friend. And of having a name chosen from family history, rather than just something plucked out of a play. And when I looked through the photo album the other day, there were more pictures of you than of me." That wasn't true, it was quite the opposite, but I thought it sounded plausible. "I counted them." I felt that I could safely move her on to a different subject. "Speaking of the photo album, did you find anything this morning? I heard you rummaging."

"I had a rootle through the drawers in the desk to see if I could dig up any incriminating evidence." If she rootled through *Lucky Jim*, she would find 5,000 euros, squirreled away in case of a nuclear war, but I didn't mention that. "I'm going to grill Dad about you-know-what this evening."

I couldn't see anyone grilling Dad about anything; he would just pretend he hadn't heard. The Gestapo would get nowhere with him; he would just smile and randomly answer, "No, no more coffee thank you," as they pulled out his toenails.

Charlotte leaned back in her chair, now almost basking in the spring sunshine. "It seems strange to think that they have been married for longer than I have been alive. Neither of us will manage that. Don't you think, by the time you are past fifty, you should be able to have a normal conversation with your parents?"

"Well, personally, I am not past fifty," I said. "Almost, but not yet."

"A normal, one-to-one conversation with them. I can't see it happening. They still speak to us as if we were infants."

"You mean that by the time you start to look like them, by the time you have gray hair and are menopausal, you should be able to speak to them on a one-to-one basis?"

"Exactly. They are as bad as each other, but in a different way."

I lit up a cigarette. "I gave Mum something to read the other day—not something I was acting in, something I had written. A short story. I wasn't asking for advice or anything; I just thought she might like to read it. All she said, at the end of eighty pages, was 'I have corrected your spelling mistakes.' "

"Well, what were you expecting? You were asking for it, weren't you? You should spend more time with Aunt Bea and less with them. You'd be happier."

"Happier, maybe. But bored shitless."

Charlotte held out two fingers. I passed her the cigarette and she took a drag, then picked up the wet dishcloth and dropped it into the bucket at her feet. "I had always imagined that there would be a moment when we would address each other as equals. Yes, I know; that sounds naïve. Or stupid. You know, leaving the mother-daughter thing behind us." She blew the smoke up into the hornbeam above. "A moment of equality, speaking to each other on level terms. How charming that would be. We would look at each other and I would say, 'Mummy, I love you.' "

I laughed. Did she think that maybe, underneath that iron exterior, Mum was all sweetness and light but just didn't show it? Perhaps she was like a lobster: all hard shell and pincers, but inside the flesh is sweet.

Charlotte passed the cigarette back to me. "When you're little, you're dependent on your parents. But as you grow up, the fear creeps in that at some point *they* will become dependent on *you*. Twenty years of looking after your own children, and then just as they have finally left home and you can do what you want, your parents start to fall apart. It would be nice to have a few years of freedom in between the two. A few years of *not* caring. Not caring, and not caring. For others."

I pinched out the cigarette and put the stub in my pocket. "Do you want another?"

Charlotte didn't smoke. (She wouldn't, would she?) Except that is when I was there. She would start by "having a puff," then move on to "sharing one" before simply helping herself out of the packet.

"Yes, let's," she said, lighting up. "Dad's terrified of becoming dependent. Not just dependent on us, on anyone other than himself. I can't imagine him being looked after. Or worse—cared for."

I couldn't see that either. "I did sort of talk to him about that. As much as you can talk to him about anything, other than cricket or the crossword. The other day, we were chopping wood in the garden. Well, *he* was chopping wood; I was putting the logs in the wheelbarrow. You should see him wield the axe! He'll be eighty in a few years, but he still chops himself into a sweaty frenzy. Or a frenzied sweat. He's clearly aiming for a sudden heart attack, hoping to drop dead, axe still in hand, and that no one will be around to resuscitate him."

Charlotte laughed and said, "Naturally, he presumes he will be the first to die, not the other way around. He might end up caring for her; can you imagine that?"

"No. I can only imagine homicide in that situation."

Charlotte was still clinging on to the cigarette. It was good to see her being bad, once in a while. She suddenly realized it and passed it to me. "Here, you have it. So you think that there will never be a brief moment of equality? We'll have to go directly from being spoken down to, to wiping their bottoms?"

"We're not there yet. You have the whole week ahead of you with Dad, and I have our trip to Paris—and thank you for staying here to look after the house."

"You see? Once again I am the one who is being abandoned. He won't say anything to *you,* but he told *me* that he's really looking forward to going to the theater. I found him reading the book you gave him, you know, the *King Lear* with you on the cover. He sounded almost proud. He also told me—"

My phone rang and I looked at the screen. It was a number I didn't recognize. I answered and there was a long silence, then a few beeps and clicks. And a chirpy voice at the other end. It was Mum. The conversation was brief and to the point. She hung up before I could say goodbye.

"Give me a drag on that." I drew long and deep on the end of the cigarette, which crackled as it neared the filter. I looked up at Charlotte with narrowed eyes.

"What?" she said. "What does she want us to bring tomorrow? The cat? A shepherd's pie? The Bible and complete works of Shakespeare?"

"She doesn't want us to bring anything. She is bringing herself. Here. You heard me. She has checked out. She is coming home tomorrow."

We went back inside and found Dad just opening his eyes and coughing. We told him the news and watched as his brain chugged and whirred like Boswell.

"Ah, yes, I see . . . Much as I suspected. Well, I'm very sorry to miss *Lear*. It was just too good to be true."

"You could still go . . . ," said Charlotte.

Dad snorted. "Yes, of course I *could*. But I won't, will I?"

"Never mind," I said. I gave a dry laugh. "You wouldn't have heard anything anyway, would you?"

"No, but I was looking forward to getting sloshed afterward." He put both hands on the armrests and levered himself up. "Right. Let's do the ducks, shall we?"

◆

Oxford, June 1964

Dear Kitty,

When I woke up yesterday, I felt that something wasn't right. I was all sticky between my legs, and when I put my hand there it was blood. DK already had his coat on and there didn't seem any point in saying anything to him. And after all, what could he do?

I washed and then went and found some pads at the back of the chest of drawers—I had put all that away thinking I wouldn't need it for a while. There wasn't that much blood really, but it didn't seem right, so I took a book and went to the clinic. I asked to see the doctor and Marge told me to wait. I went to the lavatory and had a look and there was no more blood, so I felt as if I was making a fuss about nothing. I had read half my book before I was shown in and I was right; I had made a fuss about nothing. The baby's fine, she'll come out when she's ready, which should be soon enough, and they sent me home with a stern warning about wasting the doctor's time.

Once I was home, I made a cup of tea. I washed some clothes in the sink, squeezed them out as hard as I could, and hung them up to dry on the clotheshorse. Then I started to feel dizzy. Before that it had been hurting, but in the same way as a period—you just get on with what you have to do. But now it was quite different; I can't explain. This, I said to myself, must be what pain is. Cold, hard, unforgiving. Like drifting in the sea, pushed about by the waves, and then all of a sudden one breaks over you and takes your breath away. For a moment, you are submerged and have no idea where you are, which way is up, and which way is down. I kept thinking about what I had been told; I mustn't waste the doctor's time. I said it over and over to myself: I mustn't waste the doctor's time, I mustn't waste the doctor's time. I hung on as long as I could, but by the afternoon it was too much; I went to see the landlady and she called an ambulance. I said that I could walk, it's only just around the corner really, but then a wave of pain hit me and I sat down on the stairs and knew I couldn't move. The ambulance turned up and they put a blanket around me, picked me up, and carried me, like a parcel. The landlady said, "Goodbye! Good luck!" She said she would tell DK when he was home. She waved and smiled and then they shut the ambulance doors and we left.

They put me on a drip and wrapped me in a crackly paper gown. It was dark by now and I asked if DK was there yet, but the nurse said, "You don't want anyone seeing you like this, do you?" There was a hot pipe running down the wall next to my bed and I held on to it. I held on so hard I thought I would wrench it off the wall. I waited all night and my hand was red from the pipe, but the pain just went on and on. The nurse came back in the morning and said, "We all have to go through this; don't think you're anything special," and then the doctor came in and looked between my legs and said, "Not before lunchtime." Then they all went away again.

On one side of me was the wall—all mustard yellow and peeling paint—and on the other side was a woman having her fourth baby. She was the same color and texture as the wall. Her husband was a bus driver, so I didn't talk to her. What would we have to talk about? Instead, I thought I should go through some poetry in my head. Think of something beautiful, soothing, romantic, I told myself. I tried to think of Keats, but all that came was "The Jumblies." It was "Far and few, far and few," on and on in my head. I was in the sieve with the Jumblies, being pushed around by the waves, and I made it as far as "The water it soon came in, it did, the water it soon came in," and then the pain washed over me.

The doctor was right. I looked at my watch and it was past twelve when they wheeled me out and along the corridor. By that time I had forgotten all about the Jumblies and was just saying over and over through gritted teeth, "Come on, Charlotte, come on!" And then I think they must have given me gas, or morphine, or perhaps they just clonked me on the head to shut me up.

When I woke up, I was still on my back with my legs in the air and it was cold, very cold. There were people walking around and I could hear voices, but no one even looked at me. I must have gone to sleep again, because the next thing I knew someone was shaking me and saying, "Here, you must swallow this." The nurse gripped my shoulder and made me sit up. I said drowsily, "What is it?" and she said, "Just a pill." "No," I said, "I mean, the baby." "Oh," she said, "I'm sorry, but the baby's dead. Now take your pill. Don't make a fuss or you'll wake up them that have babies to look after."

They said that DK wasn't allowed in to see me, but he wouldn't have wanted to come; he would have been embarrassed. And I suppose I was too. The next day they said I could go home—I didn't want to stay there anyway; two nights was quite enough. I didn't see the doctor, but I asked the nurse what had happened. She said it was just one of Nature's things, that I should move on and not cry about it. "Can't I see her?" I said. And the nurse said, "Her? Oh no, it was a little boy, not a girl."

It was a beautiful day and I needed the fresh air, so I walked. I went slowly and it wasn't far, but even so I felt quite light-headed by the time I was home. I took down the washing, folded it up, and put it away. It was quite dry after two days. DK came home in the evening and we didn't talk about it. He was very kind, and made toast, but he didn't say anything. Which I was glad about since I didn't want to talk about it either, ever.

I had worried about what I was going to tell everyone back in Hereford, and when, but now that's solved, isn't it? Kind Unk is the only one who knows. And you too now, Kitty.

DK is going to Greece next month, for the summer; he wants to see an inscription in Delphi. Byron wrote something about the great, green swathe of olive trees stretching from the temples to the sea. But all he wants to look at is a bit of dusty stone. He said I could come if I wanted to, but that I would probably find it a bit boring.

The landlady says she needs the room for her sister so we have to move out. There's nothing here I want to keep except for the little clock in its box, so I'll just take that and my suitcase and go home for the summer. I can help HQ bottling the plums (she says it's a good year) and the boys will be there, so it won't just be the two of us in the house. I can sit out in the pony field and play knockheads with myself.

Tuesday

Dad stayed indoors when Mum was delivered early in the afternoon in a taxi. The driver parked by the gate, got out, opened the boot, and we took out a folded wheelchair, her little suitcase, and a pair of sticks. I paid him and then, seeing his face, gave him a large tip. He smiled, climbed back into the seat, and he had let out the hand brake before we realized that Mum was still in the car. There followed a complicated scene with Charlotte, me, and the driver all suggesting the best way of extracting her—with me translating the driver's suggestions into English for Charlotte, and then re-translating Charlotte's scorn for his suggestions back into French for him. In the end, the two of them pushed from one side and I pulled from the other. She didn't slide easily on the gray velour seats—if the hospital had put a groundsheet under her, it would have been simpler. I opened out the wheelchair and pushed it to the car door, then leaned inside to grab hold of Mum and pulled.

"Tip her up!" I shouted. I had her halfway out when I caught the wheelchair with my foot. It skidded and then rolled slowly backward down the driveway. I stuffed Mum's head back in again, ran to the end of the drive to recover the chair, pushed it back up the hill, and put its brake on this time. We started the whole business over again, this time successfully.

The taxi drove off at top speed. Mum, now in the wheelchair, insisted on keeping her sticks grasped in both hands and crossed on her lap while Charlotte pushed. I watched and remembered Charlotte striding toward me at the airport on Sunday, her Samsonite suitcase gliding behind her on its well-oiled wheels. Now it was Mum on wheels and Charlotte behind her. I bent down, picked up Mum's buckled-up brown canvas suitcase, and carried it inside.

Dad and Alice were nowhere to be seen, so we parked her by the sitting room window and left her there while we went to make tea.

When we came back from the kitchen, the radio was playing from the iPod around Mum's neck, but she was asleep. I put the tray down and we turned to go. The floorboards creaked under my feet and she shifted and spoke softly. "'This wind blowing . . .'" She opened an eye. "'Not with this wind blowing.'"

"What wind, Mum?" said Charlotte.

"James?" She rubbed her eyes. "Oh! It's you. 'Not with this wind blowing, and that tide.' It was running through my head, like water. It's Kipling." She turned and saw the tray. "Tea, lovely!" She picked up the sticks and put her hands on the grips. "I'll get up for tea."

She struggled to get out of the chair and Charlotte dashed over to stop her. "Hang on, stay there; we'll bring the tea over."

"I'm quite all right now, with my sticks." She suddenly sat back down again and the wheelchair would have spun away under her weight if Charlotte hadn't grabbed hold of one of the armrests. "Ohh! I'm just a bit wobbly after the anesthetic."

"Did the doctor say you could get up and move around like that?" I asked. "I can't believe they let you out so quickly."

"And without warning us," muttered Charlotte.

"I told them not to," Mum said proudly. "Sit down, you two. When you've poured the tea." We stayed standing up. "Hang on; I'll just turn this off." She looked at the iPod. "It's *Desert Island Discs*, but really, it's not what it used to be. They invite the oddest sort of people. People I haven't even *heard* of." She put her glasses on, held the iPod out at arm's length, and prodded the screen. Rather like me on my phone, I thought miserably. "That's better. I often think about what I would have, when I'm lying in bed trying to get to sleep. Like counting sheep. People choose some very strange records. Music I can't imagine wanting to have on a desert island."

"That's not really the point, is it?" I said. "I mean, isn't the idea more that you choose the music that defines your life, that says something about who you are?" Mum looked blankly at me. "I mean, you don't necessarily just choose what your favorite records really are; you choose the ones that give the interview shape. Music that makes the program interesting. Like punctuation, between chapters."

"No, Miranda. You choose the records you would take if you were stuck on a desert island."

"When I was little, I used to think that they really did send them to a desert island," said Charlotte rather sheepishly.

"How whimsical."

Charlotte pulled the pack of cigarettes out of my hand, flipped it open, and lit up. "Well." The smoke curled up over her shoulder and mingled with the spiderwebs in the chandelier. "How did you feel when you woke up, after the anesthetic?"

"It's funny you should ask. I had an odd dream. Very clear. Like a film. I was back in Salisbury, it was a hot afternoon, and I was in the greenhouse, not asleep but drowsy. It was after lunch and there was a smell of geraniums and turpentine. I was lying on those green velvet cushions we had in the garden. They were made out of the nursery curtains. I was holding James in the crook of my arm. He was quite still, quite asleep." Charlotte and I rolled our eyes and mouthed, *Bloody James again!*, but Mum went on, "I looked up and there was this long, brown snake letting down its head, hanging there, just over me." She held out one arm, as if it was the hanging snake and her hand was its raised, questioning head. "It let down its head, very slowly, and looked at the two of us. Odd how things come back to you."

" 'A snake came to my water hole, one hot, hot day'—" I began.

"*Trough*, not *hole*," Mum cut in.

"If you say so. My water *trough*. You used to read that to me."

" 'The strange-scented shade of the great dark carob tree.' A carob tree, that was what grew in the garden in Salisbury. I know it all," she continued. " 'He trailed his yellow-brown slackness soft-bellied down, over the edge of the stone trough.' "

Charlotte leaned over on the windowsill and tapped the ash into the box hedge below. "I didn't know you could remember that. Harare, I mean, not the poem," she said.

"*Salisbury.* It was Salisbury then. Of course I can." Mum looked sure of herself, then suddenly confused. "But I don't think we had a greenhouse." Charlotte turned to me and mouthed, *She was only a baby; she's making it all up.* Mum carried on, "I'm fine now; the snake has gone away. I just have to go a bit slowly."

Charlotte grinned and brightly asked, "Did you see the hospital nurse before you left?"

"When do you start the physiotherapy?" I said.

"They should have looked at the stitches," Charlotte went on. "To make sure they're not infected."

Mum waved an impatient hand at us. "You two, you do make a fuss; it's not as if I'm handicapped, is it?"

We both looked at the wheelchair and then at each other and said, in unison, "Well, yes, it is," and giggled.

"Where is Alice? You said she would be here. What's the point in coming if she doesn't show herself? And what have you two planned for dinner?"

"I don't know what we'll have for dinner; you didn't give us much warning. We could always have eggs; there are hundreds of eggs."

"Eggs?" said Mum. "Your father won't approve of that. Eggs aren't a meal."

"He can have what he's given, can't he? For once. What would you like?"

"Yes," said Charlotte. "Why don't you choose, Mum?"

She hesitated, then said, "We'd better have some sort of meat. Otherwise he'll be cross."

"I'll go into town when we've had tea and get something from the butcher's. He'll be open today, won't he?" I said. Charlotte looked at me and narrowed her eyes. I shrugged. "I'll make you an omelette; is that OK, Charlotte?"

"Oh, you and your meat thing," said Mum dismissively. "You'll be gluten-free next. No one was allergic to gluten in the Blitz, I can tell you."

"Let's have something a bit festive," said Charlotte. "It's not often the whole family is reunited. All five of us."

"What about hemlock soup?" I suggested.

But Mum had other ideas. "There's some *blanquette de veau* in the freezer. There isn't much, but the sauce is quite rich and Charlotte seems to want eggs. There'll be enough for four, if you water it down."

◆

Oxford, November 1964

Dear Kitty,

Summer was so strange, so surreal. Everything was just as usual in Hereford, but smaller, insignificant. HQ knows that I married DK of course, but she doesn't know about anything else that happened, the rest of it—not the beginning, the middle, and not the end—and I certainly won't tell her.

Now and then a postcard from DK turned up—he was in Epidaurus, Corinth, Delphi. Always written with the same broad-nibbed fountain pen and always the same picture on the front—a chipped inscription, an armless statue, a dusty pot. And always—more or less—the same dry message.

In August I had a letter from our old landlady; her sister had decided not to come in the end and the little flat was empty if we wanted it. The Baby Belling was still there. And so here we are, back to square one: the same two rooms, the clotheshorse, the room at the back, and liver for breakfast.

Term has started again, with DK but without me. He is now a junior fellow, not an undergraduate anymore. The way things turned out I could have gone back to college in October after all, but I didn't want to be a nuisance and change everyone's plans. Next year will come along soon enough, I told myself.

But now it looks as if next year will have to wait another year because I'm pregnant—again! My life—it's all snakes and no ladders.

xxx

◆

Dinner was almost over. The ducks were in bed, the wineglasses were half-full, and cheese was still circulating. Mum was at one end in her wheelchair, her sticks propped up against the table. Juno sat next to her, licking her creamy lips. Hodge was by the door, waiting for Dad to give him an extra supper in the kitchen without Mum seeing. She picked up her wineglass and held it out to me. "Thank you, Miranda." I filled it, once again. "Alice, are you really going back with your mother tomorrow? You've only just got here."

"Yes, I have to; I've got a lecture."

"Oh yes, you and your chemistry. I didn't see much of you, did I? Make sure you've collected all your stuff together. There was a charger lying around in the sitting room. And a book of yours on the stairs."

I knew what book she was referring to. Just before dinner, Dad had been reading my *Lear* and I saw him put it on the stairs to go up to finish it in bed. "No," I said, "that's for you. I brought it down with me."

"I saw that. It's your *King Lear*, isn't it?" said Charlotte supportively. "And you on the cover—how exciting."

Dad, at the other end of the table, cut a large slice of Roquefort and put it on his plate. "At least I can read the book, even if I never got to see the play."

I looked Mum straight in the eyes. "I thought you might be interested. In my adaptation. With me on the cover. My name and my photo."

"Oh, I see. Well, it can stay here if it must." She looked at Dad attacking his Roquefort and then put her hands on the edge of the table as if she was about to get up. "Now, if you've all finished . . ."

Dad slid the cheese from his plate back onto the board and put his crumpled damask napkin down on the table. He stood up and waved a hand at Mum. "No, no, you stay here. Charlotte and I will do the washing up." Mum took her hands off the table and sank back into the wheelchair, while the rest of us got up. Dad pointed at me and Alice with his cheese knife. "You two. Keep your mother company. Or your grandmother. Both of them."

Alice picked up her plate. "I'll clear the table first."

I was not to be beaten. "Can't I wash up too?"

Dad was willing to negotiate for once. "Alice can wash with me. Miranda, you take your mother to look at the stars; she'll like that. She will no doubt tell you about them. You can wheel her out."

"I am here, you know," said Mum from the other end of the table. "I can hear you." But, for once, no one paid the slightest attention to her.

Charlotte was already halfway out of the door. "I'm washing, not drying."

"'Not washing but drying.' Isn't that Stevie Smith?" said Mum to herself, as we all frantically jostled for a job in the kitchen.

The end of dinner used to be a military organization. Dad always washed, there was no question about that; washing up was a man's job. He would stand and run hot water into the deep enamel sink, squirting dark green Fairy Liquid from shoulder level, as if he was making a cocktail. Meanwhile, Charlotte, still in school uniform and with the long plait in those days, cleared the table and piled up the dishes on his right. I stood on the left of Dad and dried up as he passed me the still-soapy plates (he wasn't a great believer in the powers of rinsing). Mum would tidy away the leftovers and put them in the fridge. I once picked up a saucepan to dry and found a large smear of mashed potato inside. I handed it back to Dad, complaining, "Do you call that clean?!" He took the pan from my hand, gave it a cursory look, and answered, "No. I call that a saucepan. But I'll wash it again if you really want me to."

Forty years later and we were still washing up, but I didn't see why we should follow the same rules. "Dad," I said, "you always *used* to wash, and we always *had* to clear the table and dry. That was in the old days, when we did as we were told." I looked around me, but Dad had gone, along with Charlotte, Alice, and both cats, through to the kitchen. We could hear the chink of crockery and water running. I was alone with Mum now.

"Kitty never did as she was told." Mum finished her glass of wine and refilled it herself. "When she was in primary school, she got up on the table and sang. Mrs. Watson told me so."

"Mrs. Watson?" I said. "Mrs. Watson was my primary school teacher; is that who you mean? But who is Kitty?" She didn't answer. "I didn't have a friend called Kitty, did I?"

"It's not always all about *you*, Miranda."

"Well then, did *you* have a friend called Kitty?" I asked. "Who is Kitty, Mum?"

There was a distant screech from the kitchen that I recognized as Charlotte laughing.

"They seem to be enjoying themselves. Well then, it's just you and me, Miranda. There's a very good moon tonight. Gibbous."

"Shall I wheel you out?"

"In a minute, yes." She wiped her mouth and then slowly and carefully folded her damask napkin, rolled it up tight, and slid it into the silver ring. "Kitty. Kitty was my sister. I haven't thought of her for years."

"Your sister? But—" I thought better of it. "Go on."

"You see, it was just me and the boys. They were much younger than me, John and Matthew. We more or less lost touch after Charlotte was born, other than funerals and Christmas cards. My mother was as tough as old boots. In those days we were brought up to write a diary. Every day, before we went to bed. It was a bit like saying your prayers, which we didn't do of course; we weren't that sort of family. It wasn't that I didn't know *what* to write in my diary; I didn't know *how* to. Where to start. I knew how to write a letter; we were taught to write thank-you letters at school. So after a while I started to write my diary as a letter, and it was much easier that way. But I had to write the letters to someone, and I didn't know anyone. I didn't really have a friend. So I invented an older sister—Kitty—who I was writing to. Kitty was always full of good advice, but she wasn't boring. She was a bit naughty—or perhaps I made her do the naughty things that I would have liked to have done. She had butter *and* jam and she was very wasteful with the toothpaste. One night she even crept downstairs in her nightie and ate all the dried apricots in the larder. I could tell her whatever I wanted; I knew she wouldn't let on. Late at night I read poetry to her. She liked Edward Lear, but then she always did have rather doubtful taste, poor Kitty. And then, when your sister was born . . . Or maybe it was a bit before that, actually . . . Well, maybe I simply didn't need Kitty anymore. She vanished, just like that, and I was on my own again." She clicked her fingers and turned to look at the sky. "And now I think we could go and look at that moon, if you don't mind giving me a push. I'll take my glass with me."

I gave her the wineglass and wheeled her as far as the French doors and the stone steps down to the garden. I put one hand on her shoulder and gave it a little squeeze. I couldn't find the brake with my foot and it was too dark to see, so I looked over her shoulder to be sure she wasn't too near the edge. "I don't think we can go any further," I said.

"I don't think we need to," said Mum, with one hand on mine. Her fingers were puffed up like sausages and her wedding ring was almost invisible. There were a few seconds of silence; then she took her hand away, changed the tone of her voice, and went on briskly, "I did suggest to your father that he put a plank down on the steps, but he hasn't done anything about it."

"You told him not to bother."

"He could have done it anyway. Never mind; we can stay here. I can see the sky if I lean forward."

"Well, don't fall out." I shifted the wheelchair again. "There, can you see the moon like that? Don't wriggle; I haven't put the brake on."

She craned her neck up at the stars. The moon had just appeared from behind the lime trees, three-quarters full and gleaming like wet cheese.

"You know, we watched it on the telly."

"Watched what?"

"The moon landing. The first man on the moon. You wouldn't remember; you weren't born. We watched it on Uncle Edward's television because we didn't have one. Kind Unk, we used to call him. We all sat around and watched it as it happened. It was terribly exciting. I was only nine. Black-and-white, of course."

"Aren't you confusing it with the first man in space?" I wasn't good at dates, but I knew that Mum wasn't nine when the first man had walked on the moon.

"No, I'm talking about the moon landing. It was, oh . . . 1952, '53, something like that."

Just then, Charlotte came in and started noisily piling up the remaining plates. I asked her when she thought the moon landing was.

"I can only vaguely remember it . . ." She paused, a stack of dirty crockery in her hands. "The early seventies, I suppose, or maybe before. Why?"

I didn't answer and she went back out into the kitchen, crossing paths with Alice, who came in and began wiping the table mats. "You see, Mum?" I said.

"Really! What does your sister know? She wasn't even born then."

"That's the point; she *was* born."

"What wouldn't Aunt Charlotte know?" asked Alice. I explained and she answered straightaway, "It was 1969."

"Oh come on, Alice!" said Mum. "Next you'll be telling me that you were born then too. You're far too young to know things like that."

Alice didn't contradict her grandmother. She went on slowly and methodically wiping the table mats.

"Let's ask Dad what he thinks. He's not too young." I called out, "Dad! Dad?"

"There's no point in asking your father what he thinks; I *know*. I was in my school blazer, and we all sat on the sofa and watched. No, that's not right: I was in my nightie; it was late at night. With Uncle Edward, I told you."

Dad came back in just then. "Glasses? Any more glasses to wash?" Standing behind Mum, he put one hand on the back of the wheelchair and raised a slippered foot behind him, as if he was about to kick a football. With a theatrical glance at me, he mimed pushing Mum off the edge. Then, with an overly sugary voice, he asked her, "Should I put the end of the blanquette in the fridge, or leave it out for the cats?"

I asked Dad when the moon landing was. He took his hand off the wheelchair, looked dumbly at us, and began to back away. He could sense danger.

Charlotte came back in and took her phone out and said to everyone in general, "I put my money on 1971, but I'll look it up." She sat down and became absorbed in the screen.

Alice put the sponge down and said, "I bet 1969."

"Dad?" I said. "Your turn." He stood like a rabbit caught in a car's headlights. I asked again. "Dad?"

"What would you *like* me to say?"

"The truth, Dad, if you can," I said. "When do you think the moon landing was?"

"The moon landing? Neil Armstrong and . . . who was it?" He looked from one to the other trying to guess what the right answer was. Charlotte still had her head bowed over the screen. He suddenly took a plunge. "Alice is right. 1969. In the summer. July."

"You see?" I said to Mum. Dad instantly knew that he had chosen the wrong answer if it was marital peace he was looking for.

"Your father doesn't know anything about space."

"Yes, actually, I do." We all turned and stared, stunned. Dad had never contradicted her before. He was steaming merrily up shit creek and had thrown his paddle overboard. "It was Apollo 11. July the twentieth."

"Apollo 11. Yes, that's right," said Alice.

"No! No! I can *remember*!" Mum was suddenly in the minority. She sounded enraged but confused.

There was no stopping Dad now. "Neil Armstrong, Buzz Aldrin, and . . . the third one was called . . ."

"Yes, what was he called? . . . They were all American, weren't they?" I said. "What was he called, the third one? He's the one everyone forgets, the one who didn't walk on the moon."

"You're all wrong!" Mum waved her wineglass furiously at the moon but caught her sleeve on the arm of the wheelchair and the glass slipped out of her hand. Red wine drenched one side of her cardigan, ran through the seat of the wheelchair, and then dribbled and splashed onto the floor.

"That's right," Dad said. "They made him stay in the lunar capsule." He picked up one of the napkins on the table and started dabbing at the puddle of wine.

"Not with damask; it will never wash out!" shouted Mum as she wrenched the napkin out of his hand. "You silly old sod."

Dad didn't flinch.

Charlotte held up her hand and looked up from her screen. "It was Michael Collins." She scrolled down, still reading. "July 1969. Michael Collins. There's even a cocktail named after him."

"Yes, a Michael Collins, of course," said Dad. "We drank those in Boston, didn't we?"

"Michael Collins! A cocktail!" Mum threw the wine-soaked napkin in his face. "How . . . How . . . American!" She stuck one stick on the ground and struggled to get up out of the wheelchair with rage. "Just the sort of thing an American would invent! Just the sort of vulgar drink That Woman of yours would know how to make! That bitch Barbara!"

Her stick slipped on the mossy step, and although I stuck a hand out as quickly as possible, the wheelchair shot away from under her and she tumbled down the steps, headfirst.

Wednesday

It had taken all four of them to get her grandmother back up the steps and into the wheelchair. The drink had numbed the pain and apart from a few bruises and a cut lip she seemed to have survived the fall. They wheeled her into the music room, put out the cats, and turned off the lights. No one said anything.

She was still asleep the next morning when Alice went to look at the chickens. She lifted the roof of the coop and shooed the Gris de Touraine out of the house. Four pale brown eggs sat on the hay. She scooped them up and placed them, still warm, on top of the corn in the bucket. She sank her hand into the cool grains that trickled and tickled against her fingers. The bucket swung from one hand as she walked across the damp lawn and back to the kitchen door, under the dusty vine.

Her grandfather was in the kitchen by the toaster, cutting up a stale baguette for the ducks. "How many?" he asked as he scraped the chunks off the board and into an old ice-cream pot.

"Four. Shall I number them?" she said.

"Four? Are you sure?" He looked into the corn bucket. "Oh bugger. That's too many."

"Too many?"

"That means your grandmother must have forgotten to do them yesterday . . ." He paused, then went on, "They only lay two a day at the moment."

"D'you mean that Grandma wanted to go all the way to the chicken run, in her wheelchair?"

"Yes, I know, it was ridiculous. But she said she was going to do it and at the time it didn't seem worth contradicting her."

"Well, what does it matter anyway?" said Alice.

"I don't want her to know."

"But she does know. I mean, she must know that she forgot to get the eggs."

"Oh, I know that she knows *that*. But I don't want her to know that I know that she forgot." He said it again, to be sure it made sense. "I don't want her to know that I know that she forgot." He put the bread knife down. "It's not the not-doing that matters; it's the me-knowing about the not-doing. But what is good is that I now know that she doesn't know that I know that she forgot." He went back to his bread chopping while Alice analyzed his explanation.

She sat down, the corn bucket on her knees, and peered down at the eggs. "Yes, I think I get it. You know that she forgot, and you also know that she doesn't know that you know that?"

"Yes, exactly. It's knowing what you don't know that makes a difference in life." He put the bread knife down again. "For once," he said, rubbing his hands together in glee, "I will be one step ahead of her." He pointed at the eggs. "You see why you can't come back with four? It's too many. Put two of them on the compost heap."

Alice didn't move. Even to her, this seemed a bit crazy. "Grandpa . . ."

"Believe me, it's easier that way; you'll see. In the long term. According to a medieval tale, Aristotle let his slave Phyllis ride him sidesaddle. Although of course Phyllis was a young, seductive creature. Not quite the same here." He weighed the ice-cream pot in one hand. "That should do for today. Put it out by the back door, will you?"

He held the pot out for her, but Alice didn't move. She thought for a while and then suggested, "In chemistry we have the periodic table with all the elements that exist. Or at least all the ones we've found so far. You can mix two elements together and get a reaction and in theory, if you know what you are doing, you can predict the outcome. You know that if you put potassium in water, you get an exothermic reaction. Heat. But people aren't like elements. People are . . . complex. They don't follow rules, however much you would like them to. You can only guess their reactions. And usually you're wrong."

"I was never wrong in the good old days. I was right but thought I had to prove it. Prove it to other people, not just myself. It was exhausting. Being right and having to prove it made me angry—with other people, not with myself."

"What? So it's easier to be wrong?"

"Yes. As long as you know you are. You see . . ."

He seemed on the verge of saying something. Something that he wasn't quite sure about himself—he, who was always sure of everything. "Last night, Michael Collins . . ." He put the pot of bread on the table and sat down next to her. "How can I explain? It was all such a long time ago. I thought that it would make things easier, more restful, if I wasn't as angry. If I stopped resisting. If I let her win—like Aristotle and Phyllis. Yes, she would have the reins; at least she would think she had. I would let her be right about something. But I would know that she was wrong. So I let her put the wrong answer in the crossword."

"Grandpa, what are you talking about? What has the crossword got to do with the moon landings? You were right about that; it *was* 1969. And it *was* Michael Collins in the lunar capsule." Alice could feel her grandfather hesitating, on the brink. "Hang on." She went out into the hall and listened. There was no sound from along the corridor where her grandmother was sleeping. She could hear her mother and her aunt cackling in the bedroom upstairs. She put one hand on the banister. She considered going up to the laughter, leaving her grandfather to his silent bread chopping. Then she turned around, came back into the kitchen, and shut the door behind her. He hadn't moved; he was still sitting at the table but now had the pot of duck bread on his lap.

Alice sat next to him. "So. Michael Collins." He looked up to the ceiling, then over his shoulder. "No, don't worry; they are all quite busy or asleep."

He drew his breath. "I meant Michael Collins as in the cocktail. As in . . . the sort of woman who would know how to make one."

"Oh, I see. That. Why is that the wrong answer in the crossword?"

"I am sure your mother and your aunt have told you about it. What they think they know about that." He picked an apple out of the fruit bowl and gently rubbed the dirt off one side with his broad thumb. "When my friend Barbara was a bit hysterical and had to go home suddenly."

Alice was embarrassed. She half stood up and put one hand on the pot of bread on his lap. "Shouldn't we take that out to the ducks?"

"No, sit down." He took her hand off the pot. "I will tell you what happened. Some things skip a generation." He shifted uneasily in his chair and played with the apple, rolling it from one hand to another. "So, Barbara. Barbara was a colleague of mine; we'd met in America a couple of years earlier. She was on sabbatical and stayed with us in the house in Oxford, the house where your mother was born. She had the room in the attic; it must have been freezing up there, but she never complained. Or at least, if she did, I've forgotten. And she didn't care about doing the done thing. She did as she pleased—as you can imagine, your grandmother didn't approve of that.

"She had been with us for several months and even I could tell that there was a certain froideur in the air . . ." He paused, put the apple back in the fruit bowl, then went on, "I don't know why, but your grandmother was out when the phone rang, so I answered. The phone was in the hall, on that ugly little table we still have. Your mother and your aunt were in their room. They must have heard some of what went on. And no doubt imagined the rest. Anyway, for once, I was the one who answered the phone. It was Barbara's brother, calling from somewhere in Arizona. There had been an accident. Barbara's husband had had a car accident and was in hospital. Barbara was right up at the top of the house, in her room, so I called her and started climbing the stairs. She came down and we met in the middle, on the second-floor landing. I told her what her brother had said. She was very upset and I'm . . . I'm not very good at that sort of thing."

"No, you wouldn't be," Alice agreed.

"Barbara wanted to fly back to Boston as soon as she could, so I went back downstairs and rang the travel agency to change her ticket. There was a flight the next day, late in the morning. Then I came back up again and told her what I'd done. There wasn't really anything else to say, but I could see that Barbara wanted me to . . ." He paused, searching for the right word. "She wanted me to *comfort* her. But I didn't know how to do that, how to comfort someone. So I shut myself in the lavatory and pretended that I couldn't hear. She knocked and knocked, but I just sat there, perched on my throne. She rattled the doorknob, but I had drawn the bolt. I coughed once or twice. Was that meant to comfort her in some way? I'm not sure. Then I sat in silence until she had calmed down and I heard her going back up to her room. When I think about it now, it was rather cowardly of me, wasn't it?" He looked at Alice, but she said nothing. "When your grandmother came home that evening, she could see that something had happened, but she never asked me exactly what. So I didn't tell her. She just presumed that what she had always suspected was right."

"But if her husband had had an accident, then why . . ."

"The husband, yes, I can't remember what he was called. But he had a beard." He picked at a loose thread on his shirt cuff. "Why didn't I say anything? Well . . . Later that evening, on the landing, when she finally accused me . . . It just seemed . . . a good opportunity. It was too good to be true. Your grandmother was always very suspicious of Barbara. No, not suspicious, she was jealous. Barbara was an attractive, bouncy sort of woman. Clever too. And easy to get on with. Happy. And so I just . . . well, I agreed with what I was accused of. I didn't even lie about it. I didn't need to."

"So you confessed to something you hadn't actually done?" Alice was beginning to understand.

"Well, I didn't *deny* it."

"But you know what really happened. You are the only one who knows." The truth settled on Alice like a gentle dusting of late snow. "And me too, now."

"Yes, it's the knowing that matters. And real power lies in knowing what you don't know." He stood up and went over to the breadboard. "You're going back today, is that right?" Alice nodded. From behind the toaster he produced a Jiffy bag. "I've got something for you." He gave it to her. "Here, it's just a book I thought you would like. Open it when you're home." She turned the thick envelope over in one hand. "Oh, and I've put a newspaper cutting in there that might interest you, inside the dust jacket. And remember—"

"Yes, always remember what you *don't* know. I will."

He nodded and slowly went up the stairs to his room at the top of the house.

◆

I was in my room packing and Charlotte was sitting on the bed. I had to leave before lunch to be in Paris in time for the evening performance. I had spent three nights in La Forgerie, more than usual, and I was itching to get home. I had been wrong about it being better going together; in the end it had been worse sharing the time with Charlotte than going as a lone spectator. Mum was already back to her usual self—it would take more than general anesthesia to change her.

"Well, it's done, but it wasn't easy, was it?" I said.

Charlotte laughed. "Denying that the moon landing was in 1969 was particularly good."

"The moon landing?! What about the mad screaming? She's never actually said That Woman's name before. And then falling down the garden steps in a drunken stupor. At least we now know the truth."

That morning we had snuck down to look at the photo album together. Both of us had already searched—individually and unsuccessfully—for the elusive photo of Barbara but were both sure that the other hadn't looked properly. And we were both right. On the sixth page there was a black-and-white photo of a younger version of Mum and Dad in bobble hats, leaning against a fence with a donkey in the background. Neither Barbara nor the bearded Sweetiepie was visible, but when we looked more closely we noticed that the white border that framed the picture was only present on three sides. The fourth side had been neatly scissored off, the picture stuck back in again, carefully re-centered on the page in its new format, the offending parts disposed of.

Alice came in, looked at the two of us and the half-packed suitcase, then asked what time we were leaving.

"As soon as possible!" I pointed at the Jiffy bag she had in one hand. "What's that?"

"Oh, just a book from Grandpa."

"Do you want to put it in the suitcase?"

"No, that's fine; I'll hang on to it."

She had been downstairs in the kitchen with Dad. I wondered what they had talked about but didn't ask—I knew that Charlotte would.

"Did he say anything to you about last night?" asked Charlotte.

"No, not really," said Alice.

"He must have said something." Charlotte wouldn't let the matter drop. "We saw you come in from doing the chickens. You were in the kitchen together for ages!"

"There were only two eggs."

"I'm not interested in eggs. What about Barbara! Did he say anything about Barbara?"

"He didn't have his ears in; I don't think he really heard anything I said." Alice pointed at the suitcase. "If we're going, I'll go upstairs and say goodbye to him properly now." She wandered out again.

"Damn," Charlotte said to me. "I thought she might have picked his brains a bit. *You* could pick his brains, if you tried."

"What? Because I'm the favorite one?"

Charlotte checked her watch. "I'd better go and see if Mum's awake. She'll want to say goodbye before you leave. Shall I take your suitcase down?" I shook my head and she left.

I made sure I hadn't forgotten anything in the bathroom. I could hear Charlotte in her sensible, low heels clip-clopping downstairs and then along the corridor to the music room where we had put Mum to sleep. Back in the bedroom, I set the sheets straight, fluffed up the pillows, and looked under the bed. There was a single sock (not mine) and a mountain of fluff and dead insects (not mine either).

I stretched out on top of the duvet, fully dressed and in my shoes. I guiltily put my feet on the bed. I thought about the *King Lear* that I had brought down with me and that was still sitting on the stairs. Or the short story that I had given Mum to read. Charlotte was right; I did ask for it. But what was the point of having children if you weren't interested in anything they did, at any point in their lives? Dad said, "Children should be seen and not heard." But what he really meant was "*not* seen and not heard."

I didn't think that Charlotte was right, about me being wanted and not her. Surely neither of us was wanted; we just happened. They had felt some sort of moral duty to feed and water us, but none to encourage us, or think of us as separate human beings that might one day be on the same level as themselves. I stared at the ceiling and thought of fatherless Alice above, silently saying goodbye to her grandfather. Was it better to have an angry father, or to have none at all?

Charlotte came back in and put a hand on my suitcase.

I rolled over onto one elbow and said, "Do you think that it will be the same for us, when we start hoarding money and smelling of pee? Do you think our children are waiting for their moment of equality?" Charlotte didn't answer. "I always hope that I have been a better parent to Alice. Better than ours were to us, I mean. But probably not. You always get it wrong, don't you? I have a theory about growing up and getting old. A) You have children; they are dear sweet little things in frocks. You think, 'Oh, how sad it will be when they grow up and leave home.' Then they *do* grow up, and become revolting teenagers. Fortunately, they then leave home and you are delighted. B) You have parents that you look up to and admire. They are cleverer, stronger, and richer than you are. You think, 'How sad it will be when they die.' Then you grow up and discover that in fact they are embarrassing, drunken bigots and you are quite pleased when at last they shuffle off. Of course both your parents *and* your children have their own agenda of A and B."

Charlotte looked at her watch again and began to wheel my suitcase toward the door. "Have you seen the time?"

We chimed together, "You can't *see* the time. Ha-ha, yes, thank you, Dad."

Charlotte sat down next to me on the bed. "Do you think we were a disappointment?"

I thought before answering. "No, not a disappointment. To be a disappointment they would have to have had some expectation of something better, and I don't think they ever expected anything of either of us. Or maybe Mum just didn't expect us—she didn't know she was expecting, I mean. It's not the same with Dad. He just agrees to whatever she says to make things easier."

"You're always on his side," said Charlotte. "You always let him get away with it. Why do you forgive him and not Mum?"

"I don't forgive anyone; what is there to forgive? They were parents. They just happened to be ours."

"You can't choose your parents, but you can choose your husband," said Charlotte. "And we both got that wrong, didn't we? At least, I did."

"I don't think that changing your mind is getting it wrong. It's just that—changing, growing up, moving on. You were brave. You had the guts to admit you didn't want that life anymore."

"At first, it wasn't easy, being on my own. But now . . . ," said Charlotte. "Now I don't want anything from men. After all, in a couple of years, men won't want anything from me, will they?" She ran a finger along the top of the bedside table, leaving a clean, dust-free track behind her. "But Dad . . . he could put his foot down sometimes. He's only henpecked because he can't be bothered not to be."

I stood up, took my suitcase, and we went out into the corridor. "Sometimes he gets what he wants. He got Barbara."

◆

Alice climbed the stairs. Her grandfather wouldn't come down to say goodbye; he didn't believe in all that soppy nonsense. On the floor below she could hear her mother and aunt laughing together. She didn't think that they were cruel, but they were perhaps unfair. Judgmental. She went into the study with its smell of cold tobacco and dusty books. Her grandfather had his back to her and was sitting bolt upright at the computer screen and typing with one finger.

Her great-great-grandfather had fought in the Dardanelles. Her great-grandfather had been something in the Foreign Office and had been posted in Palestine, then out in Africa. They had survived unharmed, but they had given their best years to the war effort. Her grandparents, born during the war, were scarred by rationing. They had turned having to "go without" into an art and they were destined to hoard all their life. They hoarded not only the present (anyone who stepped inside the larder would see that) but also the past with newspapers, photos, Christmas cards all kept, as well as more anonymous items such as old tennis balls, empty tobacco tins, and a large collection of floppy disks from the eighties.

Her mother and aunt were from a generation that had given nothing, sacrificed nothing. They had only taken. In twenty or thirty years, would they turn into her grandparents? No, probably not. They were not children of the Empire. They did not think the English better than others, nor Britain great. They did not think that women should be housewives at the beck and call of their husbands. Quite the opposite. But in time, as the lenses in their glasses grew stronger and their arms weaker, they too would find themselves laughed at as they laughed now.

Her own father had been no more than a fleeting moment in her mother's life. She knew that he was not forgotten, but he was the past. Her mother drove on relentlessly, living in the present. She would say, "Curtain up, curtain down. That's life." This didn't make Alice feel any less loved; after all, she was part of that present.

If her grandmother's motto for starting out in life was "Find a husband. Hang on to him," her mother's would be "Find a husband. Let him go." And what about her? Well, she would say, "What would I want a husband for anyway?"

Her grandfather didn't hear her coming and it was only when she put a hand on his shoulder that he turned around and smiled.

"Oh, you're off, are you?" he asked.

She nodded.

"Do you know, I had a strange thought in the night. Something that I had quite forgotten came back to me. Years ago, before your aunt and mother were born, your grandmother used to call me DK. Not DK as in 'tooth decay,' but as in the letters, a *D* and a *K*. She stopped calling me that when we were married and never called me anything ever again. 'DK' stood for 'Dog Killer.' Because of that dog, when I was learning to drive. I was a Dog Killer. I had quite forgotten that. Odd thing, memory, isn't it?" She nodded. "Don't forget the Jiffy bag, will you?"

"I have it safe in my rucksack, Grandpa, thank you." She waved a hand at him and left him to his slow and philosophical typing.

Downstairs, her mother was already waiting outside in the car. The engine was running and the passenger door was half-open. Alice threw her rucksack onto the back seat, then looked again at the house. The crest of her grandmother's white hair was just visible above the windowsill in the corridor outside the sitting room. She was waving one of her sticks at them. On the top floor, Grandpa was standing at his study window, a ghostly Quint in his tower. He stared down at her, then turned and disappeared as he drew the faded curtain across the windowpane. Her aunt stood in the front door, a dustpan in one hand. She waved goodbye with the brush in the other and then called out, "You see, you're abandoning me again!"

"Rubbish, I'll be back on Sunday! No, I mean Monday!" her mother called back. Alice got in beside her and pulled the car door shut. Her mother eased the hand brake off and the car slid slowly downhill and away.

◆

Oxford, January 1965

Dear Kitty,

Another New Year. Do you think that I have got what I wanted, or what I deserve? I'm not sure. He always gets what he wants, other than passing his driving test, because he doesn't want anything much other than his work. Does he want this baby? I don't think so. But I'm not sure he really wanted me or if he just thought he should have me. I seem to have set out on a path that I didn't really choose and am incapable of leaving, so I busily try to convince myself that that is what I really wanted. A bit like in a restaurant when the waiter asks, "Is everything as you wish, madam?" and you just smile thinly and say yes. Even if the soup is cold. How English.

The nurse said, "You have to move on," but I do think about what happened. I think about it every day. I didn't even get to see him, after all those months he'd been inside me, all that time we had been together. When I think I was convinced he was a girl! But he was my boy. My boy James.

When I was sixteen, Kind Unk gave me an edition of Kipling. The complete works, twenty little volumes, each the size of my hand. I'll leave you with something I read last night:

"Have you news of my boy Jack?"
Not this tide.
"When d'you think that he'll come back?"
Not with this wind blowing, and this tide.

"Has anyone else had word of him?"
Not this tide.
For what is sunk will hardly swim,
Not with this wind blowing, and this tide.

"Oh, dear, what comfort can I find?"
None this tide,
Nor any tide,
Except he did not shame his kind—
Not even with that wind blowing, and that tide.

Then hold your head up all the more,
This tide,
And every tide;
Because he was the son you bore,
And gave to that wind blowing and that tide!

I don't think I'll be writing to you anymore, Kitty; there is nothing left to say.

Epilogue

Scene IV

A week later, they are in the sitting room.

—Maybe it's the anesthetic, but ever since the operation I have had great swathes of poetry coming back to me. Things I learned at school, and had quite forgotten I knew. Other things too. It suddenly came back to me; you with slices of liver in your coat pocket.

—Slices of liver?

—You sound like a parrot. "Slices of liver." In our first flat, you know, Walton Well Road. I mean, after Charlotte was born. The landlady cooked you breakfast. She always made you a great slice of liver that you hated. You used to wrap it up in newspaper, put it in your pocket, and give it to my mother when you came to stay at the weekends.

—What newspaper was it?

—I don't recall.

—It's a very good story, and it's true I didn't like liver then. But I don't think I ever went to stay with your mother. All the way to Hereford? Why would I have done that?

—To be with me and Charlotte. You still had that horrid brown mackintosh that you adored for reasons known only to yourself.

—I thought we were supposed to forget things, as we got older, not dredge them up.

—No, you forget *recent* things. You dredge up the distant past. Those things are stored in different bits of your brain, and as one part rots the other part grows and fills the gap.

—I don't think I can remember the past any more than I can the present.

—When I think, all those things we learned by heart!

—I like having all that Shakespeare stored away, but most of the other stuff, lots of things we learned, were pointless—the times tables, or the order of English kings and queens—

She recites, quickly and easily:

—"Willie, Willie, Harry, Stee
Harry, Dick, John, Harry Three
One two three Neds, Richard Two
Harrys four, five, six, then who?"

—Yes, you *know* all that, but knowledge is not wisdom. What use is it knowing all the kings and queens? You could just as well look it up on the iPad.

—If you charged it up occasionally, yes, I could.

—What about seven eights?

—Oh, I was never any good at maths. It's the poetry that bubbles up.

She starts reciting to herself, at first slightly hesitantly, relying on the rhymes for the words to come back and beating the time on the arm of the sofa with one finger.

—"I am: yet what I am none cares or knows
My friends forsake me like a memory lost
I am the self-consumer of my woes
They rise and vanish in oblivious host"

He puts down his pipe and gets up.

—"Like shades in love and death's oblivion lost
And yet I am, and live with shadows tossed—"

He slowly walks toward the door.

—It's fifty-six.

She doesn't look at him. He leaves.

—"Into the nothingness of scorn and noise
Into the living sea of waking dreams."

◆

The following Monday, I took the train to Poitiers. I had ordered a taxi from the station since Mum still couldn't drive. As Dad said, "You may not want to come, but, look on the bright side, you are less likely than usual to be killed in a car accident on the way." Before the operation, when I had been there in February, she had picked me up at the station and I had offered to drive on the way home. She had refused to get out of the driving seat: "It's not far enough to be worth changing seats." I wondered how far you have to go, for it to be worth not dying.

I was in the kitchen making dinner for the three of us. Mum and Dad were in the sitting room, in the last rays of the pale spring sun. Hodge was doubtless on his stool and Juno on the sofa, both waiting for their tea. The Bad Cats roamed outside, optimistically hoping for a door to be left open by mistake.

Dad came into the kitchen and as he opened the door I could hear Mum's voice rhythmically reciting something; " 'And sleep as I in childhood sweetly slept . . .' " Dad sheltered in the doorway, listening. " ' . . . Untroubling and untroubled where I lie . . .' "

He quietly shut the door behind him, extinguishing her voice. "Hello. What are seven eights?"

"Fifty-six," I answered.

"Yes, exactly. Thank you. Now, I think we should have a quick drink, to celebrate the end of Operation Fortitude." He bent down and took a bottle of champagne out of the fridge. "We certainly deserve it. You didn't commit matricide and I avoided uxoricide. Although I did consider suicide for a moment. There was a wide selection of 'cides' available, and we avoided them all." He pulled the foil away from the neck of the bottle and started to pick at the wire cage. "At least she's not back at the wheel yet."

"What do you think will kill you first?" I asked. "Dangerous driving, drunkenness, or a heart attack from being generally angry?"

"I think a mix of all three will finish me off at some point. But I expect rage to be the leading factor. I'm not angry with other people, not anymore. There is no need to be. I am now enraged by myself. By my mistakes, by my incapacity to see them and do anything about them. Mistakes I made in Act One but always refused to see. The rest of the time I am just a cantankerous old fool."

"Admitting that you are wrong, seeing and accepting your own mistakes, that's so difficult. Of course, if you think you didn't make any, you don't need to accept them."

"Your mother and I . . . The two of us are just so bloody stubborn. We had a long and complicated exchange about poetry the other day. We were both absolutely sure we were right, as usual. And for once, I put my foot down. As I do, occasionally."

"Occasionally, yes."

He stopped untwisting the wire but kept a thumb on top of the cork. "It was to do with the bit of Verlaine that was used as the code for the D-Day landings. You know—'Les sanglots longs des violons de l'automne—' "

I finished the stanza for him, " 'Blessent mon cœur d'une langueur monotone.' "

"Ah, yes, you see, there's the rub. '*Blessent* mon cœur.' Your mother said it was 'blessent mon cœur' and was quite uppity about it. I was quite sure it was '*bercent* mon cœur.' So sure in fact that I actually went and looked it up, and bugger me, she was right. It was 'blessent.' I was sure that I had read 'bercent' somewhere. I couldn't have just invented it; I have no imagination. Then it came back to me—it was in a Churchill biography. I went upstairs to look for the book, thinking, 'Silly old sod Churchill, he got that wrong.' Well, he had and he hadn't, and so had I. It turns out that Verlaine wrote 'blessent' but that Radio Londres decided for some obscure reason to change it to 'bercent' for D-Day."

"So you were both right. Even though you thought you had misremembered. You just remembered the same truth—no, a similar truth—at different stages of history."

He went back to work on opening the champagne. "A similar truth. Yes, I can hang on to that thought, thank you. 'Truth must be my dowry.' At least I am not quite gaga yet."

"It would make you very cross, if you were."

"Only if I *knew* I was gaga. It's like dying and death. It's fine being completely gaga; it's the bit when you're *going* gaga that you want to avoid. It would certainly make me more than cantankerous. I would probably be actively angry by that stage." He pulled the wire cage free and gently eased the cork out. It went with a soft and pleasing plop. "I really don't hold with the idea of hanging around until you're eighty, when no one wants you and you are no good to anyone. The tragedy of survival. Much better to achieve what you wanted before you are thirty or forty, and then sod off and die. By then it's too late to change who you are anyway. I have thought about it. I have decided that, in that situation—if I am gaga, I mean—I want you to push me off a cliff."

"A cliff? How inconvenient of you! There are no cliffs anywhere near here."

◆

Juno's head lay turned upward on her lap, her lips drawn back into a smile, her whiskers flat in sleep. She leaned over, carefully so as not to disturb the cat, and picked up the thin volume of Kipling that was always on the table next to the sofa. The soft, cool leather of the front cover was embossed with a circle. Inside the circle was an elephant's head, a half-chomped lotus flower in its mouth. The wax-thin pages fell easily open at a bookmark; a postcard. On the front was a black-and-white photograph of a statue of the Sphinx of Naxos. A distinguished, upright, catlike creature, its wings proudly held high. She ran her finger over the nubbly front claws carved in honey-colored stone, then turned the postcard over.

In the top right-hand corner: a tomato-red postage stamp with a balding man in profile and a small crown above. Underneath him: "ΕΛΛΑΣ ΔΡ. 1,50." Ah, yes, drachmas! Liras, francs, marks. Traveling was much more exotic before the euro. The postmark was barely visible. Under the stamp, in that careful, italic hand, her name and the address of the house in Hereford.

On the left, in the same handwriting;

Delphi, 8th August 1964.
All well here.
Hope all well with you?
Love, Peter.

She turned it over again and looked at the enigmatic sphinx. She thought of the great, green swathe of olive trees stretching from the temples to the sea, and of her home in Hereford and that long and lonely, childless summer. Then she slipped the card back in between the pages, shut her eyes, and sighed.

◆

Dad took two flutes out of the cupboard over the sink. He gave them a quick dusting with a tea towel and set them up on the table.

"Well, actually, it wouldn't be *that* inconvenient for you. I looked on the Michelin map, and there's a good place a bit further down the river from here. A steep, rocky overhang that should do the business. What they call a *point de vue*. You can put me in your mother's wheelchair, she doesn't need it anymore, and swoosh! I'd go very nicely over the edge."

"Doesn't that sound a bit Shakespearean?"

"Everything sounds a bit Shakespearean when you get to my age." He carefully filled the glasses, half to start with, letting the bubbles die down before topping them up. "But maybe you are right; driving me to a cliff edge would be bothersome for you. I will have to think of something else. Perhaps I could throw myself on the bonfire. A funeral pyre. I would go up in flames like that old hen the other day. Voomf! My feathers would crackle and in the morning you would find the remains of my slippers in the cold ash." He handed me one of the glasses. "Death by my own hand seems quite the most restful solution sometimes."

"Thank you for sparing me that particular filial duty," I said as I took the glass.

He picked up his own glass, raised it high, and stood opposite me, looking at me squarely in the eyes. "I am a very foolish, fond old man. Cheers."

La Forgerie, April 2019

To whom it may concern,

All those years ago I told you I wouldn't write to Kitty again, and I didn't. But who else was there to write to? No one.

Who am I? On my birth certificate it says "Salisbury," but what does that mean to me? Nothing. A word that has followed me all my life. You could say, "You were born in Salisbury? What a lovely cathedral!" and I wouldn't correct you. It makes me feel as if I fit. Somewhere. After all, maybe you're right, maybe there is a cathedral where I was born; I will never know.

What part do I play? I have had no name but Mum for fifty years. Mum. I have just looked it up in Chambers Dictionary: "Mum, adj. silent.—n. silence—interj. not a word.—v.t. to act in a dumb show." Well, that about sums it up, doesn't it?

You know how I met him and you know we weren't close. I didn't love him, but we did have a sort of understanding. I thought we would grow into each other. No, that's not right;

I thought that he would grow into me. I thought that I could make that happen. But he changed all on his own—he mellowed; he taught himself how to pretend, how to deal with other people. He has learned to act. Whereas I, so ready to please, so unsure of myself then, I have become what he was: distant and nameless. He went one way and I went the other, but perhaps our paths crossed at one point.

Poor James. I never saw him, but he has never left me. When we were little, in Hereford, Pa would take us for a walk by the river and sometimes he would point and say, "Look, children, an otter!" And if you were lucky, you caught a glimpse of a smooth, wet back slipping into the water. As fluid as the river itself.

All these years, James has been so near. He is the one who always walks beside me. I sometimes think that if I turn around quickly enough I could touch him.

All those years. Not waving, but drowning.

Back home and on her own in Paris, Alice opened the Jiffy bag and took out the book. It was called *Lucky Jim*. It was an old hardback—the spine and corners of the dust jacket were worn and softened with age and over-reading. What was it that Grandpa had said? That there was a review or something, tucked inside. She flicked through the pages and came across a brown envelope with a window. Stamped on the front, a crest and "Inland Revenue." She opened it and tipped it up—a pile of banknotes came slithering out and fell onto the floor.

Scene V

She stands at the mantelpiece and picks up the carriage clock. She runs her finger along the crack in the glass on the side. It is ugly and deep like the scar she now has on her hip. She weighs it up in one hand, then turns it over, opens its little glass door, and slots in the key. She winds slowly, gently, as she has done every week for more than fifty years.

—Seven turns and then—stop! *she says to herself.*

—Careful now! *she tells herself.*

She can feel the mechanism resisting.

—Another quarter turn . . . and there we are.

She lays the brass key on the marble behind the clock and shuts the glass door.

Another week of life has passed.

Tonight is the last *Lear*.

We are on that last-night high, a thin varnish to hide the melancholy of the end. The curtain goes down and we are hit with a mix of triumph and sadness. One minute it is all light and sound, the audience a ghostly presence, breathing with you, hung on every word, suspended in belief. Sound and light and fury. All is there with you and nowhere else. Then in a matter of minutes the house is empty, the set lit by a single bulb hanging center stage, wet costumes lie discarded on the floor—the slough of a previous life, an abandoned shell of one who is no more. The audience are in their cars, bathed in blue neon, laughing, chatting about what there is for dinner, how much to pay the babysitter.

A single hornet buzzes across the empty stage, its work done.

Everything that has been has ceased.

Acknowledgments

The author would like to thank,

In order of appearance;

C. S. Lewis, D. H. Lawrence, Maria Edgeworth, Rudyard Kipling, Plato, Wilfred Owen, Aristotle, Percy Bysshe Shelley, Algernon Charles Swinburne, T. S. Eliot, Joseph Conrad, Raymond Chandler, Epicurus, Epictetus, Edward Lear, Stevie Smith, John Clare, and Paul Verlaine.

And, here and there, the odd smattering of Shakespeare.

Also, in alphabetical order;

Suzanne Baboneau, Sarah Ballard, Catherine Barnes, Julian Barnes, Rachel Cugnoni, Nan Graham, Larry Lamb, and Veronica Miller.

And, for his unending patience, love, and cups of tea, Olivier.